In The Midst Of The Storm

His Stormchasers
Book 4

By

Ronna M. Bacon

Isaiah 54:17

No weapon that is formed against thee shall prosper; and every tongue that shall rise against thee in judgment thou shalt condemn. This is the heritage of the servants of the Lord, and their righteousness is of me, saith the Lord.

Table of Content

Chapter 1

Tugging the dark green ball cap further down over her short cap of deep auburn curls, Ryanne Stuart leaned against the lowering oak tree just beginning to leaf out. She sighed. This is not where she had planned to be today. She had had plans to run away for the day and just take some time for her. But when her older brother had asked if she could help him, she just couldn't say no. Redmond didn't often ask for help, rather being the one who helped Ryanne and their three other siblings.

She looked around, not sure where Redmond had disappeared to. He had dropped her off at the entrance to the park and then sped away, leaving her staring after him. She had shaken her head and then walked through the park, not seeing anything or anyone that worried her. She had found a spot to watch the park. She turned a frown on her face, her dark brown eyes thoughtful. Yes, she thought, that is Redmond across from me. But what is he doing?

A sudden yell from her brother had her moving, her feet carrying her towards the activity twenty feet away from her. Redmond was moving but the other way. She had confidence in her brother that he could take care of himself. It went with what they did for a living, moving into places and bringing out ladies who wanted to come home from anywhere in the world, it seemed.

Ryanne slid to a halt, then spun in a circle. There had been a fight going on here, that she knew. But there was no one around now. This is bizarre, she thought.

She heard a rush of running footsteps before she was tackled, hitting the ground hard and then not moving. Her assailant stood over her, looking around, before he reached down and picked her up, slinging her over his shoulder, and heading for the trees near them.

Redmond stopped, bending to pick up his sister's cap, and staring around, looking up abruptly as a sharp whistle split the air. He ran towards the man beckoning for him.

"Shea? What are you doing here?" Redmond stopped, his eyes on his friend, Shea Murdoch.

"I just got here. A client had asked for photographs from this particular park. I heard something going down." He pointed behind him. "This way. They took her this way."

Redmond raced after him, his voice low as he called to him. "That was Ryanne he took."

"Ryanne? As in your sister?"

"That's right." Redmond halted, his hand on Shea's arm. "There. There is she. They've just left her there. This is so strange."

Shea nodded. "It is strange. Wait, Redmond." Shea blocked his friend from moving towards his sister. "This is a set up. It has to be."

"Whatever. I need to go and get Ryanne. She's been hurt."

As the two men moved towards Ryanne, a sudden commotion from behind them had them spinning, not able to avoid being taken down by the men behind them.

They lay still for a moment before they were on their feet, heading towards where Ryanne had been.

"She's gone!" Redmond stood where he had seen his younger sister. "Shea?" He turned when Shea didn't respond. "Shea?"

"This way." Shea appeared briefly. "They went this way. Whoever they were, they took your sister with them."

"Where's your truck?" Redmond ran towards the parking lot, his eyes searching for his sister. Lord, I have no idea what just happened, but please, dear Lord? Protect my sister. I can't go through with Ryanne what we just did with Regan. Help us to find her.

Shea shoved the key into the ignition, firing up his truck, and pulling away. "Which way, Redmond?"

"I don't know. I don't know." He paused, reaching for his phone. "She's sending me a text. Now, how did she do that?"

"Which way? Did she say?"

"Yeah. Towards the lake."

The two men finally stood outside a rough block building, watching the activity around it, knowing Ryanne was inside but not able to approach any entrance.

"Redmond?   You've had experience this way.   What do we do?"   Shea stared around. "Shouldn't we call the police?"

Redmond shook his head. "Not until I know for sure she's there. And right now I'm not." He looked around, beginning to be deeply concerned. "Why did they take her?"

"I don't know. She hasn't been up to anything she shouldn't have?   She hasn't said anything?"

"No, she hasn't.   She's been withdrawn since Regan married and went through what she did. None of us have been able to reach through to her. She's doing what she has to for Dad, but I don't think her heart's in it anymore."

"No, I doubt it is."   Shea kept his voice as low as Redmond's as they watched boxes being moved into the building. "What are they up to?"

"I don't know. That building's been abandoned for years." He sighed. "What did I do?"

"What do you mean?"

"I asked Ryanne to come with me today. I heard there was a lady wanting to meet with us. I researched it, as did Dad. It was legit. At least, that's how it came through as. Now, I wonder."

"There was no lady, was there?"

Redmond shook his head. "No, there wasn't. I don't know why Ryanne moved towards the fight. That had to have been staged."

"So, they were either after her or after you."

Redmond stared at his friend before he shrugged. "I have no idea." Glancing down at his watch, he frowned. "It's been three hours, Shea. We need to get in there."

"I know." Shea watched as the activity lessened and all but one vehicle left. "Look, there's only the one man outside now."

"But how many inside?"

"That's a chance we'll take. You head for him. I'll head for the other side of the building. Whichever one of us gets inside finds her and meets at my truck in fifteen minutes."

Shea watched for a moment as Redmond inched his way forward before he ran towards the back of the building, finding the door and reaching for the handle. Lord, guide and protect us. Let us find Ryanne and get her to safety. Then, we can find out why.

His feet carried him through the door and then along a hallway, his eyes searching, ears listening. He finally stopped outside an office door, hearing movement from behind it before the door opened and a stocky man emerged. A startled shout from the man had Shea's fist connecting with the man's jaw. He stood over him for a moment before he pushed at the door, not seeing anything. As he stepped through into the room, a soft sound caught his attention and he spun before he was across the room, crouching down beside a chair, his hand reaching to raise Ryanne's head.

Anger ran through him as he saw the bruising on her face. What did they want from you, Ryanne? What was it you couldn't or wouldn't tell them? I feel that you're just entering a storm and I wouldn't want that for you.

He scooped her into his arms, his silent feet heading for the door, pausing for a moment as he contemplated the man and then headed for the back door, sliding to a halt as he heard voices. He spun. He needed to get out with Ryanne and didn't know how. He crept down another hallway, finding a door and pushing it open, bright sunlight blinding him for a moment. He ran, Ryanne hugged tight to him, heading for his truck, finding Redmond waiting, ready to help tuck his sister into the vehicle before both men slid inside.

Shouts of rage and then cursing broke through the air as Shea keyed his vehicle to life and sped away. Thank you, Lord, he thought, as he glanced down at the lady beside him, Redmond's arm around her.

"Where to?"

"The clinic, I think. No, the hospital. She needs to be looked at. What did they do to her?"

Shea shrugged, as he pulled over to the side of the road, watching as vehicles raced towards him. "Which hospital? If we go here, then they'll find her."

Redmond shrugged. "This one, Shea. We need to keep her close to home."

Shea stared at his friend. "If you say so. That wouldn't be my choice, though. I would want to hide her away until you find out what happened."

Redmond gave a harsh laugh. "That could take months, Shea. Right now, all I care about is getting her help." He stared out the window. "I just don't know if she'll forgive me or that Mom and Dad will understand."

Chapter 2

Redmond watched as his sister's head moved restlessly on the pillow of her hospital bed, worried that she hadn't yet awakened. It had been six hours since Shea had run towards him, Ryanne in his arms. The physician had not seemed that concerned, telling her family that she had a concussion from the initial tackle. The bruising was becoming more prominent on her face. Their parents had been there, finally leaving when Redmond insisted he planned to stay with her, their mother, Naomi, reluctant to, their father, Riordan, determined to find the men responsible.

What did they want from you, Ryanne? Why beat you up? I don't get that. He turned as he heard the door swish open and Shea entered, his feet carrying him to the end of the bed where he stood, watching Ryanne, a look on his face Redmond had not seen before.

"Shea?"

Shea looked up, his curiously shaded gray eyes shuttered, before he ran his hand through his dark brown hair. "Has she awakened?"

"No, not yet, but it looks as if she is starting to." Redmond was on his feet, watching as Ryanne's eyes flickered open and closed and her head moved restlessly.

Ryanne moaned, her hand reaching for her head. "What did I go and do?"

"Just tried to help me, Ryanne."

She opened one eye, squinting against the low light. "Redmond?"

"Yeah, it's me. How are you feeling?"

She snorted, causing Shea to hide a grin. "Like I was run over by a dinosaur. Where is he?"

"Who? The dinosaur?"

She shook her head and pain crossed her face. "No. Not that. Him."

"Who?"

"Him."

"Who? Him? I'm not sure I know what you mean. The man who took you?"

She sighed, knowing Redmond was deliberately baiting her. "No. Him."

Shea shook his head at his friend before he moved to stand closer to her, his hand coming out to rest on hers, stopping the movement of her fingers as she picked at the blanket. Her hand flipped over and caught his tight.

"Redmond, is this him?"

"Who? Shea? Is that who you meant?" Redmond stared at his sister for a moment before his gaze shifted to Shea. Lord, what is going on, he asked? Is he the one she's been waiting for?

"I think so. It has to be him. Don't let him leave, please? He keeps me safe." She gave a soft sigh, raising the linked hands to rest under her cheek as she turned her head towards Shea, then shifted to her side, and drifted off to sleep.

Shea stared at Redmond for a moment, seeing the laughter his friend was trying to hide and frowned at him.

"Redmond? What just happened?"

Redmond shrugged. "I would say Ryanne just claimed you."

Shea studied his friend and then his eyes dropped to Ryanne, a softening on his face that had Redmond frowning. "Did she really say that?"

"She did. And one thing you have to understand with Ryanne. She doesn't say something she doesn't mean. If she says you keep her safe, then that's how she feels." He leaned against the foot of the bed. "So, where does that leave us?"

"In Ryanne's hospital room?" Shea grinned at Redmond as he tried to gently extract his hand from Ryanne's grip and was unable to. "She has a strong grip, you know."

"She does. I told you. She's claimed you. And with Ryanne, once she's claimed something, it's really hard to get it away from her. She said as the youngest in the family, she has to hold on to her stuff as she calls it." Redmond began to laugh softly at Shea's look.

"And that's what I am? Stuff?" His head shot around and he stared down at Ryanne as her grip tightened even more. "She is just not letting go."

Redmond continued to laugh as he moved up to help his friend free his hand. "She has a strong grip when she wants to. Ryanne, you need to let go of Shea. I promise. He's not going anywhere."

Ryanne blinked as she awoke once more, staring at the arm covered with a blue plaid shirt in her line of sight. "Redmond? When did you start wearing plaid? You don't like it."

"I'm not." Redmond's voice rippled with laughter.

"But you are. I'm holding your hand." Ryanne's frown deepened.

"No, actually, you're not. That's Shea's hand you have a grip on. And he would like it back." Redmond could barely contain his laughter as he watched the look on Shea's face before glanced down at his sister, the smile softening.

"Oh. Him. No, I can't let go. He's saved me. He has to help me. I can't do this on my own. Not anymore. He'll find them and stop them. I need him." Her voice had a low sob, something Redmond seldom heard from Ryanne.

"He won't go anywhere. I promise."
The laughter had died from Redmond's voice as he shared a grim look with Shea. "Just let him have his hand back, okay? Then we can talk."

"Redmond, please?   Don't let him leave." Ryanne's voice died away and the men watched as they thought she was drifting off to sleep, before she spoke. "He wanted something. Something I don't have. I don't know where the treasure box is. I don't know what that is. Redmond? Can you stop him?"

"I will. And so will Shea. Sleep, hon. We'll talk more in the morning." He pulled up his chair, not planning on leaving, before he shot a look at Shea, sighed, shifted his chair over so that Shea could sit, and then reached for another one for himself.

"Redmond? Do you know what she means?" Shea's voice was grim and held a threat for the men after Ryanne.

Redmond shook his head. "This is the first I've heard this. Now, I wonder….." His voice faded.

"Wonder what?" Shea's eyes were on Ryanne, feeling her grip loosening and pulled his hand free.

"What was that? Oh! I just wondered how long this has been going on. I know she's been unsettled and secretive about some things. I just thought it was because of Rory, Reilly and Regan and what they went through."

Shea's eyes studied his friend, his heart raising in prayer for Redmond and his family. "Your family has been through a lot, especially with your Dad getting shot as well as Regan. Did they ever fully explain what went on there?"

Redmond shook his head. "No, come to think about it, I'm not sure they did. I know old what's his name was after Dad and used Regan to try and get to him. That really hurt Dad."

Chapter 3

The next morning, Ryanne perched on the side of her hospital bed, her hands flat on the mattress as she braced herself to stay upright. The pounding in her head had not lessened and made it impossible for her to bend over and put on her shoes. She looked up, her eyes narrowed against the light, as the door opened and a man that she didn't know entered. She knew she should be apprehensive but wasn't. She frowned. That was not like her. Lord, what am I mixed up in that I don't know about?

Shea stopped a few feet from Ryanne, his head tilted as he watched her face before he spoke.

"The nurse told Redmond you're ready to go home. He's gone to find my truck for me. He told me I had to stay with you."

Ryanne stared at him. "I'm sorry. I don't think I know you."

23

"I'm "him"." He grinned as her frown deepened. "Let me explain. You kept asking Redmond for "him" last night. We finally figured out it was me. In fact, I had a hard time getting my hand back that you grabbed on to."

She frowned. "I don't remember. I don't hold men's hands."

Shea grinned even wider. "Well, this time, you held mine. Just be warned. Redmond may hold that against you someday."

She sighed. "If you say I did, then I guess I did. I just don't know your name."

"It's Shea Murdoch. I'm a friend of your brother's." He reached for her shoes, kneeling to slip them on her feet and tie the laces to her sneakers. He looked up when he was done, to find her watching him with a frown.

"Shea? You're that Shea? Redmond has spoken of you. I just don't get where you come in."

He stood, reaching out a hand for her. "Let's get you out of here. Can you walk?"

She slipped to the floor, waiting as her head spun for a moment, her eyes closing against the pain. Shea shook his head, looked around and not seeing a wheelchair, swept her into his arms, gathering the bag on the bed into a hand, and walked from the room, heading for the stairs, knowing the movement of the elevator would not be tolerated.

Redmond watched at Shea walked towards him, a frown on his face for a moment, before he was out of the truck, reaching for Ryanne, who buried her head into Shea's shoulder. Redmond stopped, and then opening the door, watched as Shea convinced Ryanne that she really did need to let go of him and slip onto the truck seat. Shea just shook his head at Redmond, commenting they'd talk later and slid in beside her, an arm going around her as she leaned into him, her eyes closing against the sunlight. Shea reached to slip his sunglasses on her face, earning himself a soft thank you.

"Where to, Redmond?"

Redmond sat, not moving before he turned to Shea. "I can't take her to any of our places, that's a given. Not until we can determine what's going on."

"Head for my place. Mom's in for a visit, so that would work."

"It will. But you won't have your truck." Redmond headed for his place, knowing Reilly had taken his truck there. "We can switch drivers and I'll follow you."

"That'll work." Shea stared down at Ryanne. "But I'm not sure how long we can hide her."

"Not for long, that's a given. We'll figure it out. And thanks, Shea."

"For what?"

"For being "him"." Redmond grinned at his friend, before his eyes dropped to his sister. "I don't think you'll ever live that down."

Shea grinned in response. "She informed me she didn't say that."

"She did, did she?"

Shea got a glimpse of a vehicle in the mirror. "We have a tail, I think, Redmond. Just head for my place. I can give you a ride home later."

"Or I can get Reilly to come and get me. He's in town today, trying to figure out what happened yesterday."

"Somehow, I don't think we have enough information to do just that." Shea reached for the remote to the garage door, watched as Redmond drove through the open door, and then clicked on the remote to close it. "What are we to do with Ryanne?"

"We? I didn't think there's a we." Redmond paused as he opened the door for his friend, his eyes on Ryanne's face. Lord, is he the him she's been waiting for? I pray he is. He'll be good for her.

"There's a we. I got involved yesterday. I am not walking away from her. That's a given." Shea slid from the truck, reaching to release the seat belt and then sweeping Ryanne up into his arms, hearing her faint moans and then feeling her arms around his neck. He paused, his eyes on her, something breaking open in his heart, easing the feeling of loneliness he had felt for so many years.

"Redmond, can you grab her bag?" He paused. "Somehow, I think we need to search it. Will you?"

Redmond paused as he opened the door to the house, a surprised look on his face. "You think someone got to her in the hospital? How?"

Shea shrugged as he headed for the sunroom, knowing it was the easiest room for Ryanne to be in, the quietest of the house, with a small washroom off of it. He had set it up as a guest suite. He laid her down on the couch, reaching to loosen her hands from around his neck before he tucked a blanket over her. He turned, finding Redmond nearby, staring down at his sister, hurt on his face. He rested a hand on his friend's shoulder before he walked towards his kitchen, knowing he needed to find food for them all and trying to remember if he had any soup or broth in either the fridge or freezer. He paused as he heard soft footsteps and felt his mother's arms around him in a hug.

"Mom?"

"It's okay, Shea. I have soup on for you all." Shannon Murdoch stared at her son before she nodded, her heart praying for safety for him. "She's in the sunroom? Then you need to eat. Who is with you?"

"Redmond. I don't think he'll leave her for now." He turned to stare that way. "The thing of it is, Mom? We don't know why."

Chapter 4

Naomi Stuart stared at her oldest son, not believing what he had to say, before her gaze shifted to her daughter, who sat, not watching her family but with her eyes on Shea as he sat beside her.

"Just what are you saying, Redmond? You're not making sense. He isn't, is he, Riordan?" She turned to her husband, finding his gaze on his daughter.

"I'm sorry, Naomi. What did you ask?" Riordan spoke in an absentminded manner, his full attention on his daughter.

"I asked you if you thought Redmond was making sense. I don't think he is."

Riordan turned to his oldest son, a thoughtful look on his face. "I didn't catch what you said, son."

"I said that Ryanne has gotten caught into something she has no idea what it's about. That's what she told us. Shea heard her, too." Redmond's look of concern caught his father's attention, who shifted his focus to his son more fully.

"She said that? Why? And when?" Riordan turned to Ryanne, opened his mouth to speak, and clamped it close, anger washing through him. "Redmond, we need to talk. Where can we?"

Shea looked up at that point. "Redmond, my office should work. I would come but it doesn't look as if Ryanne wants "him" to move." He grinned at her as she stared at him for a moment, her mouth open before she shut it with a snap.

"What is it with you two?" Her glare shifted between her brother and his friend.

Redmond began to laugh, Shea joining him as the other three in the room stared at the three younger people, not quite sure what was going on. "You'll never live that down, hon. Count on that. And yes, "him" will stay with you."

She looked up, catching the look on her parents' faces and groaned. "Redmond, will you just shut up? I can't explain that."

"No, but I can, seeing as I'm "him". Please, just bear with me while I do? At least I'm not the dinosaur you said ran over you." Shea grinned at her, his eyes sparkling with humour.

"I said no such thing." She stared at the two younger men as they laughed harder. "No. I wouldn't say that." They laughed even harder at the look on her face. "I didn't, did I?"

"Sorry, sis. You did. You told me you were run over by a dinosaur and when you first asked for "him", I thought that's what you were asking for. Instead, it was Shea. Apparently, you think he makes you feel safe. I told him you had claimed him and that you never let what you claim go. You had finally agreed with me that the "him" you were looking for was Shea."

"I did no such thing." Her eyes were on Shea, watching the compassionate look of his face but seeing the lurking of mischief in his eyes. "Please tell me I didn't." At their silence, she laid her head back, groaning. "Redmond, get out of here, please. Take Shea with you."

"Nope, he stays. Dad and I are going to leave and have a talk. We need to figure this out, Ryanne. We need to find who did this to you.   It was a set up, plain and simple, and I was used to do that.   I don't like that, not one bit."

Ryanne hid her face in her hands as she heard footsteps walking away before a hand touched hers in a gentle manner.   She moved her fingers, peeking out, seeing Shea had moved closer to her and that it was his hand that had touched hers.

"Are they gone?"   Her voice was barely above a whisper.

His own voice low and choked with laughter, he grinned at her before he spoke. "They have.   Even our Moms.   They were muttering dire threats and then in the next breath, comparing recipes.   I have no idea what they will come up with for a meal."

Her hands lowered to her lap, she stared at him.   "Why?"

"Why, what?"   He shook his head. "We need to stop talking like this.   We definitely need longer sentences."

She stared at him until he winked before she looked down, a blush covering her face, causing him to pause, his head tilted to watch her.

Shea sighed. This was not how he had planned to spend his day. Not at all. He looked to where he had set his camera, knowing he needed to do photo editing, but not willing to let her out of his sight. That was something new for him. Lord, how do we do this?

"Ryanne? Look, I'm sorry. I didn't mean to embarrass you. You're welcome to stay here as long as you like." He rose, reached for the camera he had set on an end table, and walked away, leaving her staring after him, shock on her face that he did just that, and then with a frown, she was on her feet, following him.

"Shea? Please? Wait for me?"

He turned, a puzzled look on his face. "Ryanne? You're supposed to be resting." He reached out a hand to help her keep her balance.

"I'm tired of resting. I know. I have a concussion. I was unconscious for who knows how long. But if I stay there, Mom will begin to hover and I can't handle that. Not today. Please? Shea? Please, take me with you, wherever you're heading with that." She pointed at his camera.

He looked at her for a long moment before sweeping her into a hug, one that she returned when the shock wore off.

"I'm heading for my studio. I need to do some editing. And yes, you may come with me. I have a chair in there that has your name on it."

"You do? How did you do that?" She stared down at their linked hands, walking with him, not seeing her father standing, watching.

Riordan had come out to ask her something, and then, paused, his eyes on first his daughter and then Redmond's friend. He shook his head. What was it with his family? They had to be danger before they started dating? He turned back to the office, his eyes on his oldest son, taking in the deep auburn on his hair, the dark brown of his eyes, the strength not just physical that showed in him. *Lord, Ryanne's going through something. Two of my children have almost died on me. Please, protect her. Protect her heart. And for my Redmond? I know once Ryanne is settled with her life mate, he'll move on. I just don't know if he'll stay with me or not.*

Redmond looked up at that moment, a frown on his face that eased. "Dad, do you have a moment?"

"For you? Always. What is it?" Riordan sat, his eyes focused on his son. "Redmond?"

"Dad, with Regan out of the group now, and I know Ryanne has been struggling as well with what Rory and Regan went through, I've been doing some thinking. I had a long talk with that friend of Regan's, Abe."

"Abe? The one with the security team? What about?"

"I wanted to know what they all did. When he said they changed from going out on assignments to training with only the odd trip, I asked why. He just laughed and said his men wanted to be home with their wives and families. He agreed with them. He wants time with Emma and their son and any other children they may have." Redmond paused, at this point, looking down, not quite sure how to express himself.

Riordan waiting, knowing that Redmond wanted to suggest something but wasn't sure how to express himself or even how his father would take what he had to say. This is it, isn't it, Lord? The change in our company that I've sensed?

"Redmond?"

Redmond stared at the computer screen, not hearing his father before he looked up, shock on his face. "Dad? Ryanne is in a lot of trouble. I don't know how much or even how safe she is."

Riordan was on his feet, one hand on Redmond's shoulder as he read the email. "I don't like this, Redmond. We both searched and searched thoroughly before we agreed you would go out there yesterday. I wouldn't have allowed Ryanne to go otherwise."

"I know." Redmond buried his face in his hands. "And I just involved Shea, without his knowing it."

Chapter 5

A week later, hearing the doorbell, Shea dropped his head and sighed in frustration. He had been struggling that day with edits that weren't working, and having someone at his door just wasn't what he needed. When it rang again, he shoved away from his desk and walked through the house, stopping to peek out the door window, then opening it.

"Ryanne? You're here?"

She nodded, looking so woebegone he just reached and pulled her into a hug, the door closing them into the house. He didn't see the vehicle parked across the street, the occupants watching his house closely.

"Ryanne? What's wrong, sweetheart?"

She finally looked up, sighing. "I don't rightly know, Shea. I just needed to talk to someone and that someone can't be family. Can I talk to you?"

Shea kept an arm around her as he led her to the kitchen, pulling out a chair for her and reaching into the fridge for the juice she favoured.

Ryanne frowned at that, then looked up at him, seeing his acceptance of her being there. "I'm sorry. I'm interrupting you. I'll leave." She made a move to stand, but his hand stopped her. He seated himself, watching her closely.

"No, it's perfectly all right. It's not your fault. It's an edit that's not working out the way I want it to." He watched her closely, seeing her hands rubbing together, an action he didn't associate with her and he reached to cover them with his. "You wanted to talk. What about?"

She finally looked at him again. "I don't know what happened that day. I've asked Redmond and he just brushes it off. I need to know. Shea, will you tell me?"

He nodded. "I will. You do need to know. It is your life, and it's not fair or right that this is kept from you. First, let me pray with you. We're walking into uncharted territory, I think, and we need to seek God's protection for you."

She sighed. "I've been doing that. Praying. Reciting all the Bible verses I can think of. Finding all the hymns and songs. I just don't have peace, Shea, and I need that, don't I?"

"You do." He bowed his head, bringing his petition to the throne. When he was finished, he waited for a moment before he looked up, finding her eyes on him.

"You believe that, don't you?"

"I do. Has Redmond ever told you what happened when I was a teenager?"

She shook her head. "No. He hasn't. He won't unless you told him he could."

Shea shrugged. "It's public knowledge, some of it is anyway. When I was fifteen, a friend decided to take his parents' car. He wanted me to go on a joyride with him. I refused and tried to talk him out of it. Long story short, he ended up hitting a tree at high speed and died. His parents blamed me, even though I was not at fault. Because they are high in society in my hometown, it became untenable for me to live there much past when I graduated from high school. I left, met up with

Redmond. He's become a very good friend, almost like a brother to me." He looked down for a moment, seeing that her hands had tightened on his. "Mom and Dad are planning on leaving there in the next few months. Dad's taken an early retirement. Knowing I won't come back there to live, they've decided to move."

"That's so sad." Ryanne sat for a moment before she spoke again. "Do you think somehow whoever it is has connected you and I through Redmond? That they're after either you or I." Her words dropped off and she paled. "Or is it Redmond they're after?"

Shea shook his head. "I doubt that. It's either you or I. Did you ever figure out the treasure chest?"

She shook her head. "No, I haven't and that was just so bizarre. And you are to tell me what happened."

"I can from when I came on the scene. Redmond said there was a woman who wanted to meet with him and he asked you to go with him. She didn't show. A fight broke out and for some reason you ran that way. Before Redmond could get to you, he was distracted somehow, and when he looked back, you had disappeared. We followed you. Somehow you got a text to him. We had found you at one point but were taken down by two men who then ran. We followed, had to wait until most of the men left, and then I walked in and found you and brought you out. You were unconscious. The physician at the hospital said you had bruising on your face and a concussion. The rest you know."

"And that's all? What did they ask for?"

"You said a treasure chest. And you had no idea what that was."

"I still don't." Her hands tightened on his, her fear coming through. "I am so afraid, Shea, and that's not me. I've gone in on some pretty messy situations, and wasn't scared. This is different."

"It is, because you're the target and you have no idea who or why." He stood, pulling her to her feet. "Come with me. I'll put you to work on some of my photos, teach you what I do. Maybe you'll have an idea or see something that I don't. And then I'll take you out to dinner as a thank you."

Hours later, her hand tight in his, he walked her towards her apartment, stopping as she pulled on his hand.

"Ryanne?"

"Something's wrong, Shea. I left a light on when I came away and it's now not on."

He pulled her back with him, tucking her into his truck, and sliding in. "I have a friend I can call. He's a police officer. He'll walk through your place for you."

Shea watched as his friend approached, a grim look on his face.

"Bob?"

"Your friend knows her home. It's trashed, to put it mildly. I've called it in. It'll be a while before we can have her go through. Likely early morning. Is there somewhere she can stay?"

"I can take her to her parents or her brother's, but she won't leave. She's already told me that."

Bob nodded. "I know the family. You're right. She won't. Will she be comfortable enough in your truck?"

"I'll make sure she is." Shea turned and slid back into his truck, his hand reaching for Ryanne's.

"Shea? What did he say?"

"That you were right. Someone's been in your place. He's put in a call to report it. You can't go in, he didn't think, not likely until early morning."

She sighed. "This just gets better and better. Where is God in all this?" She pulled her hand back, wrapping her arms around herself, and staring out the side window, leaving Shea to watch her closely.

Chapter 6

Her hand tight in Shea's once more, Ryanne walked through the door of her apartment and stopped abruptly, her hand going to her mouth, as she stared around.

"Shea?"

"I know, sweetheart. I know. Let's go with the officer and you can tell him if you notice anything that's missing right off. We'll put your things back after that and reassess at that point."

She nodded and then moved away from him, standing for a moment in her living room, tears on her cheeks as she saw the destruction.

"Why?"

The police officer had been watching her and finally spoke. "This is personal, Miss Stuart. Not random. They are trying to send you a message. I understand you were kidnapped and injured a few weeks. Whether this is related to that or not, we'll certainly look into that."

"It will be. I just know it will be. And this is not the end. It wasn't for Rory or Reilly or Regan. Why would I be any different?" She moved away quickly, her feet taking her through the apartment before she stood in her kitchen, back to the wall, and then sliding down to sit, arms tight around her upraised knees, her head buried on them.

Shea had watched her walk away, and then watched as the officer left before he reached for his phone, not sure if he should make the call but knowing Redmond would want to know and would want to be there for his little sister.

He found Ryanne finally, sitting beside her and wrapping her in a hug, feeling her tears soaking into his shirt, his head down on hers. He heard footsteps that stopped at the kitchen and then moved through the apartment. Another set of footsteps sounded and he heard quiet voices, knowing that Redmond and Reilly were there and then he heard a female voice. Reilly's wife, he thought. Good, he thought. Ryanne needs a lady here.

Ryanne finally looked up, watching closely as Redmond approached and crouched down in front of her, concern for her colouring his face.

"You okay, sis?" Redmond watched his sister closely, a slight frown on his face as he saw her wrapped in Shea's arms, her head on his shoulder, and caught Shea's slight shake of his head.

She shook her head. "I don't know, Redmond. Who did this? That's what I want to know."

"I talked to the officer as he was leaving. He doesn't have a lot to work on, he said."

She shoved to her feet, brushing by him without a word. He stood and watched before he turned to Shea, who had risen, his eyes following Ryanne.

"You didn't call last night. Neither did she."

"She was safe. She refused to call you. She didn't want you involved, she said. At that point, I agreed with her. She needed space to absorb what had happened.

You would have smothered her, Redmond. You know that."

"Like we'd stay away. Rory and Leah are here. They had come by earlier today, Leah insisting that they had to. This is why. Reilly and Aideen are away, or they'd be here." He sighed. "And then we have to yet tell Dad and Mom."

"That's not going to go over well. We had a chance to talk a lot yesterday. She showed up mid-afternoon, wanting details of what had happened to her. She refused to come to one of you, said you had been refusing to tell her. It's her life, Redmond. She needs to know what happened. If she doesn't, she can't take precautions. Anyway, she stayed, I worked on my editing, and then we went out for a meal." His hand up, Shea shook his head, catching the look on Redmond's face. "As friends, Redmond. As friends. I have no idea how she made it to my place. She didn't have her car. When we got here, she stopped and told me someone had been here. She was right." He stepped to the doorway, watching as Rory and Leah worked in the living room, not seeing Ryanne.

"Is this about what happened?"

"We don't know. She has no idea what they want. She is adamant on that."

"Then, why?"

Shea shrugged. "You know my history. I know as much of yours as you can tell me." He nodded towards the bedroom area, knowing that was where Ryanne had ended up. "What I don't know is what's going on with her and has in the past. I suspect she hasn't even told her family."

Redmond ran his hands through his hair. "Another Regan, is what you're saying."

Shea turned to face his friend. "Regan?"

"Yeah, Regan. She hid stuff from us, wouldn't tell us. That led in part to what happened to her and to Delaney." He sighed as his phone chimed, pulling it out. "It's Regan. She and Delaney are here, at my place." He looked up. "Do I tell them to come?"

As he reached to respond to the text, Shea's hand on his arm stopped him. "No, Redmond. Don't make that decision for her.

I did, calling you. I should have asked her first. Talk to her. She needs to take back her life. If you keep stepping in, you or Rory or Reilly or even your Dad, she'll never open up to any of us."

Redmond stared at his friend, before his phone was tucked away in his pocket. "You're right, Shea. We just make decisions for her. We always have. Part I think because she's a lady, but mostly because she's our little sister."

"Your little sister is not so little anymore. She is trying to stand up for herself, to become the person God wants her to be. I see the struggle going on. Even when we were teasing her, I saw underneath the longing to be recognized as an individual. How you handle this? That will colour your relationship with her from now on."

Redmond stared at the living room, watching as Rory and Leah worked away, Leah stopping every once in a while to rub at her lower back. He sighed. "You're right, Shea. How did you get so wise?"

Shea shrugged. "Just by observing people, I guess. I see a lot when I'm doing photo shoots. People can't hide what's in their eyes." He looked past his friend, his eyes on Ryanne as she stood in the hallway, devastation on her face. "She's in the hall, Redmond. Go to her. Talk to her. Listen to her. Pray for her. But remember, what you do now? It will either bring you closer to her or drive a wedge between you. And that gap may never close if you do that."

Redmond nodded as he turned, his eyes on his sister before he walked towards her, stopping short of touching her. He lowered his head to study her face before she looked up at him.

"Redmond?"

"Ryanne? How are you? Other than the obvious?"

She shrugged. "I don't know, Redmond. Can we move me from here? I can't stay here."

"We can do that, if you're sure." He reached with hesitant hands, to pull her into a hug, feeling her stiffen against him, and then he stepped back, understanding what Shea had been meaning. "It's your decision, sis. What you want. Not what we want. No more of running roughshod over your wants and desires."

Ryanne stared at her brother, seeing his sincerity in his face. "You mean that, Redmond?" Her voice was a low whisper, almost as if she had been afraid to speak. "That's not you."

"From now on it is. Your defender over there? Shea? He saw something we have all missed. We've not been treating you as a lady, full grown, and able to make her own decisions. I'll talk to everyone, including Mom and Dad. Things will change. Hold us accountable, Ryanne. Don't let us run over you anymore."

She nodded, then turned back to her bedroom. "Please, Redmond? I can't stay here, not anymore."

"Where would you like to go?"

She turned, seeing Shea standing watching from the end of the hall.

"With Shea. You have keys to the door. Lock up when you leave. Just pack some personal stuff for me and leave it with Mom and Dad. Take my car there too." She almost ran down the hall towards Shea who simply swept her into a hug, a nod at Redmond, before he had her out of the apartment, leaving the three remaining staring after her.

Chapter 7

Riordan stood at the doorway to his daughter's apartment, seeing it empty, and turned to find Redmond standing beside him, sorrow on his face, but something else he could not read.

"Redmond? Where's your sister?" He flung his hand around as he entered the living room, staring at the empty room before he walked the entire apartment, the sounds of his footsteps echoing back from the cleared out rooms.

"She's given up her apartment, Dad. Where she is right now? I'm not sure. All I know she is with Shea." He held up a hand as his father spun to face him, mouth opened to speak. "Before you say anything, that was her choice. I support her in whatever steps and decisions she makes." He looked down, and when he looked up, his father stood in front of him, a frown on his face, seeing the sorrow still of his son's face.

"Redmond? Was she hurt?"

Redmond gave a harsh laugh as he jammed his hands into his pockets. "Physically, no. Emotionally? Mentally? Spiritually? She's hurting, Dad, and we never saw it. Shea did. He said she's been hiding something and she won't tell us. He said that we needed to step back, let her make her own decisions. In other words, stop speaking for her and stop hovering over her."

Riordan took a step backwards, rubbing at the back of his neck, as he pondered his son's words and his eyes slid shut. "We do that, don't we, son? We speak for her, make decisions for her, and she has just let us."

"It's the way Ryanne is, Dad. She didn't want to cause waves. Shea warned me to be careful how I spoke with her at the apartment, that if I did it wrong, I'd drive a wedge between us that might never heal."

Riordan paced before stepping through the open front door and outside, his eyes watchful, feeling someone out there. "Shea's right. We need to step back. And that will be difficult."

He turned as Redmond locked the door and then stared down at the keys. "Is she safe, that's all I need to know right now, son?"

"As far as I know, she is. Leah packed up enough for her to last two weeks or so without doing laundry. That's what Shea asked. He said he'd call tonight, just didn't tell me where he was heading. It's near here, I suspect. I know he has photo shoots upcoming that are in the area."

Riordan nodded as he stood at his car, looking in the distance. "When you talk to him, have him call me. I would like to speak with him and with Ryanne, if I can."

"I will tell him, Dad."

Riordan finally drove away. He needed to be in the office, but right now, his heart was hurting for his youngest child. He turned towards home, knowing he'd find Naomi there. This was something they needed to discuss as parents and then pray about. He had never known how Ryanne had felt. He sighed. Of course he hadn't. He had never bothered to really talk to her, not for years.

Pulling to a stop in front of a sprawling one story house, Shea turned off the ignition and waited, before he turned to Ryanne, finding her staring out the side window. She had spoken little since he had driven away from her apartment and he had let her have her silence, not wanting to push. He looked past the house, towards Lake Erie, finding it one of its calmer days.

"Shea?" He turned back to watch her. "Where are we?"

"This was my maternal grandparents' home. It was left to me. For now, Mom and Dad are moving here. We're near our town, just outside it by about twenty minutes. Once Mom and Dad are settled, I'll give up the rental I'm in and move here." He glanced in the rearview mirror. "If we haven't been followed, then we're safe here."

"But your parents won't be." She stared at him as he began to laugh. "Shea! This isn't funny."

He sobered even though laughter still sparkled in his eyes and laced his voice. "They'll be okay. Dad worked in security. Mom was a police officer."

"They were? But they're not now?"

He slid from the truck, coming around to open her door, to help her out before he grabbed their bags from the back seat. "They've put in enough years they can retire and decided that was exactly what they wanted to do. Their interests have changed to short-term missions." His key in the lock opened the door at the back of the house, leading them into a mudroom and from there into a kitchen. "Here, let me walk you through the house." He dropped her bag into a middle bedroom. "This is yours for as long as you want it. Before you ask, Mom and Dad are heading here later today."

"They are? I can't stay here. I'll bring danger to them." She turned, heading for the door, when his hand stopped her. She looked up at him. "Shea?"

"You don't have to leave. Dad made sure we had a really good security system put in. There are extensive motion sensor lights and cameras outside. Not intrusive." He paused, looking down at her, not able to continue for a moment. "I would like it if you did stay."

She finally nodded, and walked through the remaining rooms, taking a peek into the bedrooms before moving towards the living room. "This is a nice house. It's well laid out." She spun, her eyes on him, finding him standing, a shoulder against a wall. "Shea? You need to work. You can't babysit me all the time.""

He moved towards her, his fingers touching her cheek, before his hands went back into his pockets. "I know. You don't need a babysitter. You need a friend to walk alongside you. I would like to be that friend. And yet I have to work. I could use an assistant, if you want something to do. That is, unless you're going back to work for your father."

She shook her head. "Right at the moment, I'm not sure I can. I'm still off on sick leave. Dad won't let me back until I'm cleared and with the mild vertigo and headaches, that won't happen for a bit." She sighed as she found a chair to curl up in, watching as he chose a chair close to her, his eyes not moving from her. "I need to talk to Dad. And I don't know how to."

Shea cleared his throat. "I talked to Redmond before we left. Forgive me if I overstepped. I suggested to him that they needed to think through how they were treating you. He didn't realize how they were treating you, that they were making decisions for you that they didn't have the right to do. He said he would talk to your brothers and your father, explain things, and get them to agree to back off and let you live your own life without them stepping in on every single thing."

"You did that? Shea? Thank you." She was on her feet, hugging him, before sitting back down, her legs tucked up under her, her shoes on the floor. "No one has ever done that. I have prayed so much lately to be free of that, to be able to move around without feeling stifled." She watched his face. "And how did Redmond take it? Not well, I would think."

"How did he treat you at the apartment before you left?" He watched, a soft smile on his face as she thought back and then her eyes closed.

"You had already talked to him. I wondered at his comments and his conduct." She looked up. "Thank you."

Chapter 8

Standing in the kitchen, coffee pot in hand, Shea's father, Samuel, watched his son react with Ryanne, laughing at something his mother had said. He shook his head. Shea never dated, that much Samuel knew. So what was it about this young lady that had him like this? He would need to have a talk with him and he wasn't sure suddenly how to do just that. He knew from what Shea had said when he had called early that morning that Ryanne was in danger and he also knew his son would not walk away from anyone in danger, no matter the risk to himself.

"Shea? Coffee?"

"Sure, Dad. Ryanne would rather have juice." He laughed at her pretended protest before she took the glass he handed her.

"I was trying to escape this, you know. People making decisions for me."

Shea swiped the glass back from her just as she was raising it to drink from. "Then, in that case, you don't want this. You need to tell us what you want."

A pretended look of horror on her face. "Wait! You can't throw that out. I want that." She took it back, and then retreated across the kitchen to stand beside Samuel. "Your son is incorrigible."

Samuel stared at her for a moment even as he heard Shannon laughing at that and Shea protesting that he wasn't, that she had read him wrong. "He is, is he? You're not the first to tell him that." He looked over at Shea, seeing something different about his son, and prayed that he would finally be free of the burden he had carried for so many years. "Now, young lady, I understand you're having an adventure and haven't asked us to join you."

Ryanne stared up at Samuel, her eyes narrowed, before she caught the glint of teasing on his face. "I am. And I didn't think I needed to ask. People just seem to be dropping into it. And no, there was no dinosaur."

Samuel stared at her as Shea shouted with laughter. "Care to explain, son? I think your mother and I lost something somewhere."

Shea did just that, Ryanne protesting at his telling of it, adding her own perspective to it, before Shannon broke in, her arm around Ryanne. "She's right, Samuel. That's what the boys did. She's not had a moment's peace since she said that."

"Shea wouldn't do that, now would he, Shannon?" His wife just shook his head as Shea laughed, an answering grin on his father's face. "How we find our supper and then we can talk. Ryanne, you are welcome to stay here as long as you feel comfortable doing that. Shannon and I are here to stay now." He looked over at Shea as he said that. "We've sold the house, Shea. The movers will be there to pack up everything and bring it over here. Your Mom and I brought the personal things today."

"That's wonderful, Dad. I'm glad the sale went quick." Shea moved to take the casserole from the oven and place it on the hot pad waiting on the table. "Now, Ryanne, what would you really like to have to drink? We usually have tea with a meal, but your choice is just that.”

“Tea sounds fine, but what kind?” She smirked as he stopped for a moment before he grinned and pulled open a cupboard.

“What kind would you like?”

Her mouth open, she walked over. “You weren’t kidding, were you?”

“We never kid about our tea, Ryanne.” Shannon reached past her for a tin. “This will work.”

Ryanne finally sat back, flushed with laughter, her heart warmed by how she had been welcomed into the family, she thought. She looked up at Samuel, seeing his nod at her.

“Have you talked to your family today?” His first question surprised her.

“Not since I walked away from the apartment. Redmond sent a text, letting me know it was all cleared out, that my things were stored at the office in a spare unit there.” She looked down. “I’m not sure how to approach them.”

"By being yourself. Be honest with them. Shea said he spoke with Redmond and that Redmond had agreed to speak with your brothers and your father. I suspect that he has by now. Pray for strength to go forward." Shannon reached for her hands. "God does not want us living in fear, my dear. He wants us to be the vibrant positive strong person He created. We let people and things beat us down."

She nodded, before looking up at Shea's father. "Samuel, how do I stay safe? How do I stop this? And how do I not involve your family in this? I don't want anyone hurt."

"Those are good questions, Ryanne. You are thinking through the process of what has happened and what will happen. Knowing some of what your father does, I can see where you're heading. I have met your father over the years. I didn't connect him with Redmond. Not until now." He looked at her, compassion on his face. "I'll think through what I can. I may need to go to your family but I won't without talking to you first, unless and only unless you are in grave danger. Do you agree with that?"

She nodded, her eyes now on Shea, seeing something there that had a frown whispering across her face. "I guess I do need to talk to Dad. I just don't want to."

"We could do it for you, but this is one conversation you do need to have." Samuel stood, his hands reaching to clear the table. "Let's put this stuff where it needs to be. Then, Ryanne, if you will, let us pray with you? We would like to do that." Samuel paused and then walked away, returning with his Bible. "I have some verses I feel the urgency to give you, if you'll let me."

"I will. I need all the help I can get. Having seen and been part of what Rory, Reilly and Regan went through, I'm scared. I don't want anyone hurt because of me." She knew she was repeating herself but felt she had to.

Shea reached to hug her, before pulling back her chair once more and seating her, taking his mother's chair beside her and then reaching for her hands. "Dad's right. We need to immerse you in prayer and verses. God is the only one who can truly protect you. No matter what you're going to go through, we're not leaving. That's a given.   We'll help protect you from whatever "dinosaurs" you're facing." He studied her face that she had turned to him. "We tease you about that, but know that's to help you cope. Humour does help in these situations. It keeps a balance there for you. Dad and Mom have used it many times in their career. And to say dinosaur, I think you realize just how big and dangerous the situation is."

Chapter 9

Sitting at the table later that evening, her head leaning on her hand, Ryanne stared down at her phone, knowing she had to call her father, but really hesitant to. Instead, she turned the phone over and stared at the back of it. She jumped slightly as she felt a hand rub along the back of her shoulders and looked up as Shea sat, his hand reaching for hers.

"Can't do it?" His words were low, full of compassion for the situation she found herself it. "First time doing something without your family's approval?"

She sighed as she flipped her phone over. "I think it is. I feel like I'm running and Dad will question why I didn't run to them. I know he's hurting over this."

"And so are you. It's part of becoming an adult, this letting go on both your parts. He will always be your father, loving, caring, protective, worrying. That will never change. He will understand that you are grown and you need to stand on your own two feet. Will a walk first help?"

She shook her head. "Maybe later." She reached for his hand as he went to stand. "Shea? Will you stay?"

Shea sat back down, his eyes searching her, not realizing how much she was becoming to mean to him and how much he wanted to take this burden away from her. "Are you sure?" At her nod, he reached over and kissed her cheek, causing her to stare at him, her hand on the very spot. "Do you want me to talk first?"

"I would, if that's not a coward's way of doing it."

"No, it's letting a friend who cares deeply about you help." He reached for her phone, frowning as he stared at it. "Did anyone ever search it for any rogue applications?"

She nodded. "We do that on a weekly basis. It's part of our process. There hasn't been anything found. Why?"

He shrugged. "I don't know. When was it searched this week?"

She sighed, knowing that it hadn't been. "It hasn't been this week. I never thought to do it. I usually hand it over to our techs on Monday mornings."

"Then, we shut it down and use mine." He rose, taking her phone and heading for his father, asking him to search it. Samuel stared at it and then at him and nodded.

Shea sat back down, his phone extended to her. He grinned. "Still not going to?"

She shrugged. "This conversation changes things. It changes our relationship."

"It will but it will also strengthen it. Your father knows you're an adult but he hasn't let go of you being his little girl. He never will totally. That's a given." He stared down at his phone as it chimed. "It's Redmond."

"Answer it. Then, I'll call Dad."

"Redmond? You're calling me? What's up?" Shea listened, his eyes on Ryanne. "I see. She's right here. I'll let her know. Thanks for calling."

"Shea? What did Redmond say?"

"That your old apartment was broken into again. The manager called the police. There was a message spray painted on the walls, warning that you had what they wanted and they would not rest until you turned it over. He'll send a copy of the photo soon."

She nodded as she reached for his phone, pausing for a moment to collect her thoughts before she dialed. "Dad?"

"Ryanne? Are you okay, love? I've, I mean, your mother and I have been so worried. You didn't call us earlier."

"No, I couldn't, Dad. Coming home last night to what I did was such a shock." She hesitated before she continued. "I didn't want any of you hurt. Our family has been through enough already."

"Ryanne, never ever think that. You are an important part of our family and we worry about you." She heard her father clear his throat. "Redmond talked to me. His friend really got through to him. I'm sorry, love. I didn't realize that was how you felt."

"Well, it is. You and the boys always do that. Take over. Don't listen to me about my personal life. Don't let me make the decisions I need to make. It's one thing to do that with work, and even then, I should be able to express my opinion and can't." She blinked back tears. "I need time, Dad, time to process what's going on. Can you give me that?"

"We can. Your mother and I had a long talk this afternoon."

"What? You didn't stay at the office? That's what you would do!"

Riordan groaned. He had been trying to change, but sometimes forgot. "No, I felt it more important to talk to your mother. Redmond really laid it on the line. He's right. Shea's right. We need to do this for you. Can you work with us, hold us accountable if we forget? And I'm sure there will be times that we do."

"I can, Dad, but for now, I'm not coming home. I've found somewhere to stay, where I feel safe."

"Just keep in touch as much as you can. We love you, Ryanne. You are an important part of our family. Call us if you need us, no matter the time of day or night."

She clicked off the phone without a goodbye, wiping at the tears on her cheeks, before Shea swept her into a tight hug. She felt his kiss on the top of her head and felt cherished and safe. She heard his whispered prayers, not hearing the soft footsteps that stopped at the doorway or the sound of a chair sliding quietly back beside her. She jumped slightly as she felt arms coming around Shea and herself and then heard Shannon's quiet prayer.

She finally rose, heading for her bedroom, not able to express how she felt. Shea stood and watched before he turned to his mother.

"She called her father."

"And?" Shannon studied her son.

"I'm not sure. I heard her side but not his, so I can't say how it went." He sighed. "And Redmond called. Her old apartment was broken into and a message threatening her painted on the walls. I'm glad she wasn't there."

"God knew, son. He knew she needed to leave there today. She wouldn't have been around if you hadn't taken the steps you and her family did. Now, how do we keep her safe? And where does she want to live?"

Shea shook his head, a slight smile on his face. "For now, she's told her father she is where she feels safe. She won't tell him where. That concerns me, Mom. She should and hasn't."

"That's part of taking control of her life." Shannon sat back, her thoughts in a muddle. "I did the same with your grandparents. It wasn't as bad as what Ryanne is facing, but I felt I had to take a step to claim my independence. Dad never wanted me to go into law enforcement, but he accepted the fact that was what I wanted to do."

"I never knew that. Grandpa was always so proud of what you were doing."

"It took a few years and many conversations but he was won over. Now, about Ryanne. What is she planning on doing?"

Shea shrugged. "I have suggested that I could use her help on my photo shoots, but she hasn't said yes or no. What are your suggestions, Mom?"

Shannon shook her heard. "No, that's a conversation I need to have with Ryanne. And it can wait. You both need to seek your sleep, early as it is. I know for a fact you would not have had any sleep last night, not with watching out for your lady." She rose and walked away, not seeing the look of shock and the acceptance of Shea's face.

"That's what she is, isn't she, Lord? My lady. The lady I've been waiting for. The lady Mom used to weave into my bedtime stories and that she and Dad have prayed for. Keep her safe, please, Dear Lord?"

He rose, heading for the room he planned on using, stopping for a moment outside Ryanne's closed door to pray for her.

Samuel stood and watched his son, peace in his heart about his son, but worry as well. He knew only too well what the young couple could and would be facing.

Chapter 10

Frustration in her very stance, Ryanne stared across the office at Redmond. She had stopped by to talk with her father but had had to wait until he finished a conference call. Redmond had tracked her down and tried to find out where she was living.

"Redmond! If I wanted you to know, I would tell you. Now, stop! This is what Shea meant, you know." She spun, heading for the door, stopping as she heard his words of apology.

"You're right, sis. I can't stop being your big brother. It's part of me that wants to keep you safe."

She turned to him, shaking her head. "I know, Redmond. This time, you need to back away. Let me make my own decisions. When and if I want you to interfere, I'll tell you. Let Dad know I was here. I'll call him later." She was gone before he could stop her.

Riordan stared at the closing door and then at Redmond. "Redmond? What just happened?"

"All I did was ask if she was safe and where she was living? She's changed, Dad. I don't know this Ryanne."

"No, she's not changed. She is just showing us she is a person in her own rights. She always has tried, and we've ignored that." He sighed. "Did she say where she was staying?"

Redmond shook his head. "No, she hasn't. And she hasn't answered my texts."

"And just how many have you sent?" At Redmond's look of guilt, Riordan shook a finger at his son. "No more. I know you. You keep pushing and you need to back off. Let her call you, text you, email you. She will if you stop. She's done that with me. I've told her to call me if she needs us and she has, just to talk."

"I know, Dad. This is just so hard. All I can see is how she looked when Shea carried her over to the truck that day. I'll never forget that. I didn't know how bad she was hurt."

"I know, son. That's something you shouldn't have had to go through, either one of you. Has she said anything more about that?"

"No. I'm not sure she knows. And then with that warning, she's retreating more and more."

Shea just reached to wrap Ryanne in a hug as she ran to him. "Didn't go well with your Dad?"

"I didn't see him. Redmond happened." She felt his body shaking with laughter. "This is not funny, Shea. He's too intense, too in my face."

"I know. He loves you and is very worried. That's how he copes." He leaned back. "Now that you didn't see your Dad, do you want to hang around here or go find something fun to do?"

"Let's go. Something fun? What do you have in mind?" She snapped her seatbelt into place and turned as he started the truck.

"I have to do a photoshoot at a local petting zoo. Like to join me?" He grinned as she nodded, happiness flooding her face.

"That is exactly what I need. How far?"

He began to laugh and she joined him. "Not too eager, are you? It's only about twenty miles or whatever it is in kilometres. I'm old school, that way."

She shook her head at him. "That would be around thirty kilometres, my dear sir." She looked out the window, not catching his glance at her.

Late that afternoon, Ryanne scrolled through the photos on his camera, her face happy. "That was fun, Shea. No wonder you do what you do. These will make your client happy."

"It will. It's hard to narrow down the ones I need. I always take too many."

"Can I help?" She looked up at him, almost begging him to let her.

"That you can. Now, we need to eat. How be we pick up something and stop at the park near the lake? The sun is getting close to setting and there is always a gorgeous sight there."

"Sure, if we're safe."

"We should be."

An hour later, Ryanne leaned against Shea, his arm around her, and pulled down her cap, her eyes on the setting sun and the colours in the sky and the lake. "This is so peaceful, Shea. It makes me forget what's happening."

"And have you remembered anything at all?"

"Nothing. I have no idea what they want. A treasure chest? That sounds like something out of a book or a movie."

"It does, but it is a reality for you. I want to keep you safe, but I don't know how to do that."

She looked up at him, knowing how much she had come to depend on him in such a short time and that scared her. "Shea? We need to talk at some point, don't we?"

He watched her face, sighing to himself. Had he been that obvious, he wondered? "We will. Now's not the time. Come on. Let's head for home." Her hand in his, he led her to his truck, tucking her inside.

Neither one of them saw the men standing outside a SUV, watching them closely. That fact would come back to haunt them at a later date. Shea always wondered afterwards what would have happened if he had seen them.

Shannon looked up as she heard their laughter, a smile crossing her face before she glanced at the envelope on the table. She had been in town earlier that day and have come across Redmond, who had paused and then asked if she would deliver a letter to Shea. If she could, then Shea would be able to get it to Ryanne, she was asked. She had agreed, not sure if she should have.

Chapter 11

Turning from his desk, Shea watched Ryanne as she looked over the photos he had printed, setting aside the ones she really liked, discarding the ones that weren't up to her standards. He grinned, knowing how exact she was being.

He looked down at his phone as it chimed, seeing Redmond's name and number and then moved away from the office, heading outdoors.

"Redmond? You're calling me? What's up?" Shea listened as Redmond shuffled papers.

"Where is Ryanne?"

"She's safe, right at the moment. Why?"

"Because we just had a letter delivered, threatening her. Somehow, they've connected her to us and we don't know how. You know how quiet we keep our work."

Shea squinted at the sun before he sank down into one of the chairs on the patio. "I know. So how did they do that?"

"We're working on that. Is she safe?"

"She is, Redmond. Right now, she's working over photos for me."

"She is? I would not have thought that."

"See? That's what she means, Redmond. She has always wanted to do photography but didn't as she felt she needed to stay with the family business. This break is doing her good. It's letting her see another side of life, one that she desperately needs."

Redmond sighed. "I gather she's won you over to her side."

"There are no sides in this, my friend. Just Ryanne and what is best for her. And yes, Mom delivered the letter and I passed it on to her. She took a look at it and set it aside. As far as I know, she has not read it. And she will if she needs to."

"I know, Shea. It's just that it's a letter from all of us. We each wrote out a page or two, just to express how we feel." Shea heard the sigh from the other end of the phone. "Will you ask her to, for me?"

Shea was silent, wanting to help his friend but not wanting to put pressure on the woman he was beginning to care deeply for. He finally sighed. "I can't, Redmond. That's not what I've promised her I would do."

Redmond was silent for a moment before he spoke once more. "Thank you for being honest with me, Shea. You always have been."

Shea finally stood, his phone away, and walked down the yard, his eyes thoughtful as he went back over the conversation. He turned, finding Ryanne standing near him, her head to one side, a smile on her face.

"You're deep in thought."

"I am. I just talked with Redmond."

"And? I know. He asked about the letter, and no, I have not opened it yet. I am not sure if I want to."

"Just for the record, he says it has a letter from each of the members of your family. No pressure. Just that they wanted to express how they feel about you.”

“Really? That would be a first that they would do that, other than Regan. She and I have always been able to tell each other how we feel. And I know we both have had to stand up for ourselves. She did it by marrying Delaney and then leaving the family business. Maybe, that’s what I need to do. Get married and move away.”

“Run to me, Ryanne. Please? If you’re running away, take me with you.” Shea’s voice was low, low enough that she hardly heard him.

Ryanne spun, not quite sure if she had heard right. “Shea? Just what did you say? And what are you asking?”

He shrugged, not quite sure what he was asking or if she was even ready to hear that. “I value your friendship, Ryanne. I would like to be the one to help you.”

She finally nodded, moving into his space to hug him. “Thank you, Shea. I needed to hear that.” She stood, her head leaning against his arm. “This is so hard, you know? I don't want to be a danger to anyone, but I'm not sure what is going on."

"I don't think any of us know. Part of the reason Redmond called is that there was a letter delivered to your office, threatening you. They're desperate to figure out how these people knew."

"They followed us, didn't they? Isn't that what they always do?"

Shea looked down at her and grinned. "You do like your movies and books, don't you?" He ducked the elbow she aimed at him. "How did you make out with all the photos?"

"I've set aside the ones I really like. I hope they're what you are looking for."

"If you've chosen them, then they are." He watched as she turned her face up to him. "You have excellent taste in pictures. I saw that in your home."

She blew out a breath as she moved away from him and back towards the house. "Shea? What's different out there?"

"I'm not sure what you mean. I don't notice anything different."

She turned in a circle. "Something is." She walked towards the back of the yard. "Here. In the hedge. You didn't have an opening in it yesterday."

Shea stared at the hedge and then at her, before grabbing her hand and pulling her back towards the house. "We need to get you inside, Ryanne. Someone's done that on purpose."

He slammed the door, bending to stare out the window, even as he heard his mother's surprised voice behind him.

"Shea? What in the world is going on? You two raced in here like you were called and couldn't get here fast enough."

"Ryanne's very observant, Mom. Did you notice the opening in the hedge? That's new."

"Opening? In the hedge? Just what are you talking about?" She stood beside her son, peering out. "Why, there is one. Who did that?"

"That's what we would like to know. Mom, don't go out there."

She just stared him down and opened the door, marching through the yard.

Ryanne watched her, her hands clutching at Shea's arm.

Shea stood for a moment, torn as to whether to go after his mother or stay with Ryanne.   Samuel watched him for a moment, then shaking his head, headed after his wife.

Ryanne watched as the couple walked slowly back towards the house, deep in conversation, before she turned to Shea.

"I did this, Shea. I brought this danger to you. I need to leave." She spun towards the hall, intent on packing and then finding a ride, but Shea's hand on her arm stopped her.

"No, don't run, Ryanne. That's what they want you to do. They want you scared enough that you'll head out on your own." He looked around at his parents. "We need to get you to see your parents and then decide from there what we need to do."

Chapter 12

Ryanne watched her father, seated across from him in their living room, hearing her mother heading her way. She reached for Shea's hand, needing that contact with him, not sure yet where they were heading as a couple, but knowing she just didn't want to leave him or have him leave her. She was avoiding her feelings and emotions, pretending that what she felt didn't exist.

"Ryanne, did you talk to Redmond?"

She shook her head at her father's question. "No, I came to you instead. What was his urgency?"

"We received a threat today, directed at you. Redmond said he spoke with Shea."

She turned to study Shea, finding his eyes on her. "Oh, he did mention something, but then we found that opening in the hedge and that took my mind off that."

"Opening? In the hedge? Shea, what is she talking about?" Riordan's gaze shifted to the younger man.

"We found an opening in the hedge at the back of the property. Mom and Dad took a look at it. They haven't said yet what they suspected."

Riordan sighed. "And you're just telling me now?"

Ryanne drew back, tamping down her anger. "Dad, we found it, what three hours ago? How would we have known to tell you? You wanted to meet. You mentioned this threat. What is that about?"

Riordan just stared at her. "This is serious, Ryanne."

"I know, Dad. Don't you think I don't know that? It's my life that's being threatened." She made a motion to rise but Shea's hand kept her in her seat.

"Just listen to your Dad for a moment, love. Then, we can make plans. Or you can leave. It's your choice what you do."

She searched Shea's face, seeing his belief in her, his trust in her decisions, and sighed. Without looking away, she spoke to her father. "What did they threaten, Dad?"

"They were vague. They didn't specify a threat, just that you would pay unless you turned over the treasure chest." He looked down at the file he held. "And we have no idea what that is."

She shrugged as she looked at him. "I don't, Dad. I have nothing other than my own belongings. But then, if someone could break in and trash my place, I suppose someone could break in and hide something. I guess that means I have to go through all my things."

"Not today. That we can do another day, when you tell us you're ready to do that. All I care about right now is that you are safe." He shared a look with Shea before nodding, reading in the younger man his pledge to keep Ryanne as safe as he could. "Your brothers are working on this, you know."

"I know." She sighed once more. "They need to do their own work."

"They are. This has become their work for now." Riordan held up a hand at her protest. "We did it for the others, Ryanne. You are no different from them. We need to solve this."

"I know we do, Dad. I'm just not sure how we do that." She rose and paced, coming to a halt behind Shea, her hand resting on his shoulder as he reached up to touch hers. "Dad, why? What would I have? I've brought nothing back from any trips. You know that. It's part of how we work."

"I know. That's what we don't understand. This is just so out of the blue." Riordan looked up as Naomi hesitated in the doorway. "Naomi?"

She shook her head. "Nothing. Just a thought."

"And what was that, Mom?" She turned to face her mother. "Or are you going to hide your suspicions from me as well?"

Her mother just shook her head again. "No, it's just that I don't have an idea that clear, Ryanne."

Ryanne stared at her mother for a moment, before she turned back to her father, frustrated at the lack of news and the feeling she was still in danger. Shea watched closely, knowing how close to running she was.

"Riordan, perhaps if you go over all your findings with Ryanne, it will help. She needs to know what the risks are, what you have discovered, and what your thoughts are. She can't make an informed decision of what she wants to do without that." He turned to watch the older man. "This is what you do with your clients. Your family should be no different." His heart raised in prayer, hoping that he had not overstepped the boundary.

Riordan stared at the younger man, anger rising briefly before he nodded. Shea was correct, he thought. They were doing Ryanne a disservice by not speaking frankly with her. He had not done that with his sons, and even Regan had been given information.

"Ryanne? Can you sit for a few moments? Shea's right. We do need to talk." Her father watched as she slipped onto the couch beside Shea, his arm coming around her, and wondered how close these two were.

"What do you have, Dad?" Ryanne's voice was quiet. She wasn't too sure she wanted to hear any more bad news.

"There are the threats. Yes, more than one. We have told you about them, I think?" He watched as she nodded. "They are very unspecific. Vague. Almost as if it's a fishing expedition they're on."

Ryanne looked at Shea before sharing a look with her mother. "That's what I don't get, Dad. It is like they are not too sure what they should be looking for. You're right, it's just too vague." She shifted closer to Shea without realizing she had moved and reached for his hand, gripping it tightly. "I've gone back over all our trips, all our travels, all the clients that I had contact with. The only one that was so odd was the one Rory and Regan were on last. And then that one you had when we were little."

Riordan nodded, having come to the same conclusion. "We keep going back to that trip, and I don't understand why. It's like there is unfinished business there."

"There is, Dad, and I don't know what. We have been over and over all the data we have, and just don't seem to find the link we're looking for."

"Regan was sorting through the files the last time she was here. She found a number of photos I didn't know we had." Riordan's voice paused as he looked at Shea. "Shea, you are just who we need. If you look at the photos, you might see something we have missed."

Shea nodded, his eyes on Ryanne. "Do you have copies I could take with me? I can run them through my programs and see what I can come up with."

Naomi was on her feet, almost running from the room and back. "Here. For some reason, I printed two sets when Regan was here. She questioned me. I had no idea why."

"God. He knew you would ask me and prepared you to do this." Shea looked down at Ryanne, seeing the fatigue in her face. "If there's nothing more, I need to Ryanne back to safety."

Riordan opened his mouth to say she would be safe with them, then clamped it closed. Ryanne had made it obvious where she wanted to be. As her parents, they needed to step back and let her make her own choices. Lord, this is so hard, he thought. I want to protect her but have to let her go. That's what You do with us, isn't it? You let us go free so we learn to trust You more fully.

Chapter 13

Shea sat back in his chair the next morning, a frown on his face. He had glanced over the photos briefly and then copied them to a file on his computer, running a program he had designed to recognize places and people. It was coming back with hit after hit.

Ryanne sat watching him before she rose and stood beside him, her eyes on the monitor.

"Shea? You're frowning."

"I am? Yeah, I guess I am. There is something really odd about these photos. Who took them?"

"Rory and Regan took most of them. The local person took some. What are you finding?"

"People and places that don't fit where you said they were." He looked around, and then reached for a book he had taken from his shelf earlier. "See? This is the area they were in. This is what it should look like. And these photos, I am assuming the ones taken by the local, are different. The ones taken by your family match the area."

"How did you do that, Shea? I don't know how many times we've looked over those and not see that."

"It's subtle what is done. Do you know if the local person had their camera for any length of time? I'm trying to determine just how this was done."

"I can ask." She reached for her phone when Shea's hand stopped her.

"We can do that later. Right now, tell me what you want to do. Thanks to your help, I've been able to catch up on the editing I needed to do."

She perched on the corner of the desk, her toe pushing his chair into a rocking motion. "I don't know, Shea. I really don't know. I would like to go out somewhere but I'm not sure how safe that is."

"You have a choice, Ryanne. You can let whoever this is control your life and chase you into hiding for who knows how long. Or you can take back your life and do what you want to do, being aware that may mean danger. God does not want you to live in fear. Cautions and preparedness, yes. That He wants but not for you to be hiding from life."

"That's true." She rose. "I wish I had my car."

"Where do you want to go? I'll play chauffeur for you." He grinned as she spun to stare at him. "I'm not afraid, Ryanne, if that's what your concern in. I'm cautious. I know something could well happen to either one of us. It could happen here or at your place or at your parents or when you're out and about."

She nodded. "Okay. Are you sure you can leave your work?"

"I can. I'll just tuck a camera in my pocket and then if I see something, I can do a photo shoot."

They wandered through the town and then headed for a local park on the lakeshore. Ryanne stood, her face turned up to the sun, her eyes closed. Shea drew in a deep breath, realizing how much she was coming to mean to him, and reached for his camera, quickly taking photos before he tucked the camera away and reached for her hand.

She stared at their hands. "Shea? Do we need to talk?"

"About what? That I value your friendship? That I don't want anything to happen to you? That I would like to get to know you better? See where we go?"

She looked at him, finally remembering to close her mouth before she spoke. "All that? Wow! That's a lot to want to do."

"Is it? And I want to explore our friendship. You are a beautiful, talented lady that I am honoured to call friend."

She studied him, shrugged and then walked away. He could hear her muttering but couldn't make out her words as he ran to catch up with her. Neither one saw the man following or the car keeping pace with them as they walked back towards Shea's truck. He walked beside her, watching her face closely.

Sudden squealing of tires had him spinning and then grabbing for her hand as he ran for his truck, pulling her with him.

He slid to a halt as the car slithered to a stop in front of them and he backed away. He could feel Ryanne's hand tightening on his as he caught her looking around, desperate to find a way to escape. She tugged him with her, heading for the rocks near them, hoping to find somewhere to hide.

Appearing in front of them, the man pointed his weapon at Ryanne's head. Shea felt the pressure for a knife against his neck and tightened his hold on Ryanne's hand. They couldn't escape, not yet. They stood, frozen in place, not sure which way to turn. Forced towards the car, Shea's hand tightened more on Ryanne's, watching an opportunity to get away. None presented itself and fear grew within him as they were shoved into the backseat of the vehicle and one of the men jumped in, beside Ryanne, his gun pointed directly at her, a frown on his face in warning to Shea.

Shea felt Ryanne's hand gripping his harder. He could feel the fear coming from her but also the anger. He had no idea who these men were but he was determined to protect her however he could. He felt Ryanne drawing closer to him, and tightened his hold on her hand, his eyes watchful, studying the two men in the front seat and then the man beside Ryanne. He heard a softly indrawn breath and turned his attention to her, finding her staring ahead through the windshield.

He followed her line of sight and shuddered. They were heading into town and from the direction they were going, he didn't think it was a good part of town. He looked around, watching closely, praying for an opportunity to escape. He watched the men closely, his hand on the door handle, ready to spring into action.

His opportunity came as the vehicle stopped and the men stepped out and away from the vehicle, their backs to the car. He shoved open his door and with his hand clutching Ryanne's tightly, pulled her out of the car and with him. He ran stooped over until he was able to make it out of sight.

Ryanne turned back as she heard the shouts of rage behind them and then looked around, pulling him towards a street.

"This way, Shea. This way. It will take us to the lakeshore and I can find somewhere for us to hide. They will expect us to head the other way."

Chapter 14

Sliding to a halt and pulling Ryanne into his arms, Shea leaned back against the large rock pile they had hidden behind, his breathing coming hard and fast. He could feel Ryanne's breathing laboured from the run, and he knew both of their hearts were pounding. He listened but could not hear any sound of pursuit.

"Did we lose them, Shea?" Ryanne peered around the edge of the rock, being careful to keep herself hidden.

"For now, but who knows for how long." He looked around, not sure where to head. "Where now? You know the area."

She spun, her hand to her cheek, as she studied the area and then pointed. "That way. It will lead us towards town, but we'll be hidden for the most part." She grabbed at his hand and pulled him with her.

She finally stopped, leaning against the building she had found. Shea leaned beside her, his eyes on her, not sure why she had stopped.

"Ryanne?" His voice was low and she shrugged.

"I don't see them, Shea, but they're out there. I can feel them. They know where we're staying, more than likely. They know where my family is. Where do we go?" She slumped back against the building, her eyes on him, defeated for the moment.

"How do we get to the back of my place?"

She stared at him, not sure what he was asking. "The back of your place?"

"That's right. If we go in through there, maybe they won't see us."

She snorted, causing him to grin. "I highly doubt that. When we disappeared, that's where they would head." She stared into the distance, not seeing the building across from them, her brow furrowed in thought before she shoved herself away from the wall and walked towards the centre of town.

Shea stared at her for a moment before he ran to catch up with her, his hand reaching for hers. "Talk to me, Ryanne. Tell me what you're thinking."

"I am thinking we need to get back to somewhere we can call someone. Only I have no idea where that somewhere is or who that someone would be." She stopped short, throwing her hands into the air. "Where's God in this, Shea? Does He even care?"

Shea simply wrapped her into a hug, his chin on her head, as he prayed through the words he needed. She was hurting, doubting, not sure of him, not sure anymore about her family, not feeling safe and secure, and he needed to handle this right.

"Shea? You're quiet. I guess you don't know either." She tried to move away from him but his arms tightened on her as he looked around and then drew her to the sidewalk and a bench under a spreading maple tree.

"I don't have the answers you're looking for. We don't know who the men are, what they want, where they are right now. God is here, Ryanne. I have no doubt of that. He helped us to escape. We shouldn't have been able to walk away from that car, not with three armed men there. We shouldn't have been able to escape and end up sitting here. He cares so much for you, Ryanne. He understands as He placed you here, right here and now. He has a purpose for this. Only I have no idea just what that purpose is."

She watched him closely, almost not blinking, desperate for reassurance. "But why, then? Shea?"

He shrugged. "I don't know. All I know is that a beautiful lady I care about is in danger, and I can't stop that from happening, no matter how much I want to." He looked around. "How do we get away from here?"

She looked around, knowing the conversation was over and that she needed to think about his words. "This way. It will lead us to your place." She sighed. "Shea, I need to find a place of my own. I can't continue to live with you and your parents. It's not right. Your Mom mentioned a house they were buying and that there was a short closing date."

"I know. I'm trying to think of how we do this." He watched her as they walked hand in hand through town. "I won't do what I understand Reilly did. If and when I were to ask you to marry me, it would be after courting you, letting you have all the fun and enjoyment of that and then planning a wedding. You deserve that."

She stopped in her tracks, her mouth opening and closing as she stared at him. "You're serious, aren't you?"

He looked down at her, his heart in his eyes, as he nodded. "I am, and I say no more until you are ready to hear that, if you ever are. Now, where are we?"

"Standing in the middle of street, about to be run over." She ran for the sidewalk, Shea following as she ran down the sidewalk and then ducked into a store.

Shea shook his head, even as he looked around. A book store, he thought. Why? He followed Ryanne as she moved through the store, not looking right or left, and heading for the employee door, slipping through it and pulling him after her, letting it shut softly before she headed for the back door and opened it, peeking out.

"This way, Shea. We're not far from your place now." She led him once more through the streets until she stood inside the hedge at the back of the property.

"So you see anything off?'

He shook his head. "No, I don't, but then I wouldn't know what I was looking for." He led her towards the back door, unlocking it and slipping inside.

His mother looked up from where she was seated at the table, papers spread around her.

"You two are here? Where have you been?" She rose to come and hug them. "Your Dad went looking for you."

'Why?" Shea had no idea what his mother was meaning.

She reached for a paper and waved it at him, making him grab for it to stop its movement. "This. It's another threat, more detailed this time."

Shea reached for it even as his eyes flickered towards Ryanne, seeing resignation on her face but no fear. He frowned as his eyes dropped to the paper, her hand coming up to tilt his towards her so she could read.

"This is getting brutal, Ryanne."

She shrugged. "I've seen this before. Rory, Reilly and Regan all had letters like this. I have seen them at work as well." She looked up at Shannon, who was watching her intently. "Shannon, from your perspective, what are your thoughts?"

Shannon nodded. "It's getting worse, but they are still not specific. Vague threats. But what happened to you two? I know something did."

Shea pulled back a chair, shoving Ryanne into it and then reaching for coffee for them. Sitting beside her, he tucked her hand into his before his spoke. "We were abducted and then got away. It was so strange, Mom. They drove us across town and then all three men got out, standing with their backs to the car, and arguing. They didn't lock the car and I was able to open the door and pull Ryanne out."

Shannon stared at him for a moment, before she turned to Ryanne, her mouth open to speak before she closed it, watching Ryanne as she studied Shea, seeing something different in how she was looking at him.

Chapter 15

Riordan stared at his daughter as she stood in front of him, arms folded across her body and with Shea's arms wrapped around her before he looked up at Shea, seeing his determination to keep her safe in his eyes.

"Ryanne? Did they say anything?"

"Not a word. That's what so bizarre. They made us get into the car, drove us to where the burger place is and past it to park near the shore, and then just stood outside, arguing. It's as if they were waiting for someone else to come." She leaned back against Shea, feeling the strength in him. "Why?"

"That's strange." Riordan began to pace, his hand rubbing at his hair, before he stopped and spun, his eyes on Samuel and Shannon. "Where do we go from here?"

"Ryanne needs to go through her belongings, first." Samuel turned his attention to Ryanne. "Can we do that tomorrow?"

She nodded. "Dad, they're at the office?"

"No, actually. We took them to our place and tucked them into the building near the house. We were thinking that way you could go through them when you wanted and not be distracted."

"Yeah, right." She shoved away from Shea and headed for the outside. "I need some air."

Shea went to follow her when his father stopped him with a hand on his arm. "Let me, son. She may take what we have to discuss better from me. I can talk to her from a security perspective that no one else can."

Shea nodded. "She won't be locked up somewhere, Dad. She has already told me that."

"No, it wouldn't work. Not this time. We don't have enough information to know who it is." He turned to Riordan. "Riordan, can you jot down anything you can think of? Your family should to."

Riordan waved his phone. "Already done. They'll email it to me."

Samuel nodded as he watched his son. "Shea? Write down in detail what you went through today and back to when you met Redmond that day. No matter how small a detail. We need to determine who she saw or what she may have that she doesn't know she has."

Shea nodded, his eyes on the door, longing to follow Ryanne, but knowing his father was the best one to speak with her at this point.

Samuel shut the door quietly behind him, searching for Ryanne, finding her curled up in his favourite chair, her arms wrapped around her knees, watching as he approached.

"Samuel? What have you decided to do with me?"

He grinned at her, looking very much like his son. "Right now? Nothing. We'll have you look through your things, see if there's anything there that doesn't belong to you. Shannon has spoke with the detective who was assigned to your abduction and he is quite concerned.

"And your Dad and your family are trying to sort through what they know. Shea's going through what he knows since he met you." He laughed as she snorted. "Don't you think he won't?"

"No. He'll tell you to look for the dinosaur that I told them ran over me." She paused, her eyes turning suddenly thoughtful, as she looked at Samuel. "Samuel, what am I remembering? What is it about a dinosaur?"

He froze, knowing what she was asking. "You've seen or heard something that you can't quite remember and it's coming out as this, isn't it?"

She nodded. "It has to be. Is there any chance we could go back to the building they found me in?"

Samuel was on his feet, reaching for her hand. "We can and we will. Right now. Who do you want to go with you?"

She shrugged, a small smile hovering on her face. "I don't see us getting away from the three in there. Redmond would be good."

"Then, we'll have your Dad call him and he can meet us there. I had cleared it with the police that if you wanted to go through the building at any time we can. Shannon will let the detective know."

An hour later, she stood, her eyes studying the room, tracing the walls and ceiling and then the floor of the room Shea insisted she had been kept in. It had been totally cleared out.

"Shea, about where was I? Do you remember?"

Shea nodded. "Right here." He moved to a spot near the back of the room, away from the windows and the door. "Right here, Ryanne. You were here, unconscious."

"This makes no sense. This is a well known building, even though it is empty and starting to be rundown. Why choose it?"

"We'll ask them when we find them." Riordan spoke from where he stood near the door, his eyes intense on his daughter, seeing the shift in her thinking and yes, he thought, her character. She's not trusting as easily as she did and that hurts. It has to affect her walk with God as well.

"Dad? This seems familiar. Why?" Ryanne spun in a circle. "I feel like I've seen this place before."

Redmond had been watching, silent, studying the room. "It's been renovated, Ryanne." He groaned. "It looks like that room from that last trip. Are we never going to be free of that trip?"

Riordan shot his son a look before he turned to Regan. "Is that what you see?"

She nodded, her eyes on her sister. "But why go after Ryanne? She wasn't there."

Riordan nodded. "That's what I don't understand."

Chapter 16

An hour later, Ryanne stared around the room her possessions had been stored in, hand on her head, not quite sure where to begin. Shea's arm was around her shoulder, bringing her comfort as she leaned into him. Redmond and Regan watched, not quite sure what was going on with the two, but wanting to be there to support their sister.

"Ryanne?   Where do you want to start?"   Redmond's question had his sister turning to him.

"I'm not sure, Redmond.   I didn't pack, so I have no idea what is where."

"We labeled the boxes for you, Ryanne."   Regan walked towards one and pulled it over to her.   "This is from the living room. It says pictures."

"That sounds like the best one to start with then, doesn't it?"   Ryanne dropped to her knees, her eyes on the box, when she felt Shea's hand on her shoulder.   She looked up at him, a question on her face.

"We need to pray first, love. Ask for guidance and wisdom, and yes, protection. Redmond, will you?"

Ryanne listened as her brother prayed for them, not quite sure how she felt anymore. This adventure as they persisted in calling it had shaken her faith, her trust, and who knows what other emotion.

She finally looked down, staring as Shea's knife sliced through the tape and he folded back the flaps. She hesitated and then reached for the first photo, Shea's hands there to take it from her. Photo after photo was removed, until the last one, one that she held on to, staring at if for a long time before she looked up at Regan, a bleak look on her face.

"Regan, do you remember that friend we had? Mary?"

"I do, Ryanne. Why?" Regan was on the floor beside her sister, arm around her as she studied the photo. "This is her. I didn't know you had a photo of her."

"I didn't. This isn't mine. So why do I have it?"

Redmond shared a look with Shea and then studied the photo. "Mary? She's the one who drowned and they never found the body? You were there, weren't you, Ryanne?"

"I was. I tried to find her but couldn't. We all did. They could never decide what actually happened." She looked up at her brother. "Is she still alive? Is she behind this?"

Redmond's face grew stern and he nodded. "It's always a possibility. She was your age, right, Ryanne?"

"She was." Her face paled even more. "Her parents never forgave me. They blamed me. I thought Mom and Dad had talked to them."

"Let me have her full name and birthdate, sis. I'll look into it. I'll talk to Dad, too." Redmond walked away, his phone out as he called their father.

Shea crouched down beside Ryanne, reaching for the photo. "There's a dinosaur in the background, Ryanne. Did you notice that?"

"What? Where?" She stared at him before she reached for the photo. "There is. I know that place." She scrambled to her feet, Regan beside her as they ran for the door, Shea on their heels, Redmond spinning to follow, tucking his phone away.

"Where are we heading?" Redmond's question almost stopped Ryanne in her tracks.

"To the Rocks. There's a dinosaur in the photo. That photo was taken there. Shea, can you tell if it's photoshopped at all?" Ryanne tossed him the photo.

"She looks your age now, Ryanne. How is that?"

"I don't know, and I don't like it. We need to figure this out and so that quickly. I feel such a sense of impending doom." She slid into his truck, watching as he keyed the motor to life, her hands on the photo. She knew Regan and Redmond were behind them.

Ryanne stood staring around, not quite sure where she should be heading in the park. Shea's hand reached for hers, pulling her along with him, his eyes searching for anything that stood out. He finally pulled them to a stop in front of the dinosaur that Ryanne had recognized.

"This is it?"

She nodded. "It is. It's a new addition, within the last three years." She shared a look with her siblings. "That's about right, isn't it?"

"It is." Redmond agreed, even as he pulled out his phone. "Dad's found some information already. He says that the authorities were convinced her drowning was faked, but they could never prove it. He also says there have been sightings rumoured to be her over the years in this area."

"That's so bizarre, Redmond. She always seemed happy and content. Her parents were strict but not outrageously so."

"No, they weren't." Regan spoke up, even as she moved around the dinosaur. "I don't see anything here that would stand out or mean anything, do you?"

Ryanne shook her head, even as she watched Shea's eyes narrow and saw him reach for a spot. "Shea?"

"This? I don't think this is meant to be part of the original statue." He pulled a packet matching in colour to the statue from it and handed it to Redmond. "I think we need your team to look at that before we do."

Redmond shared a look with him before looking at his sister. "We will do that. Anything else here? If not, let's get Ryanne out of sight. I don't like the feeling I have."

Chapter 17

A month later, Ryanne stood in her new apartment, looking around, not quite sure if she had made the right move. Her parents had asked if she had wanted to move home but she shook her head, stating she needed to do this. She had to take back her life, didn't she? She could tell they had not been happy with her but had acquiesced to her statement.

Shea stood for a moment just inside the front door, watching Ryanne as she finally moved around, his heart in his eyes before he shuttered them and walked towards her, his hands coming up to stop her movement.

Ryanne looked up at him, a frown on her face. "Shea? What are you doing here?"

"You let me in, remember?" Shea frowned as well, realizing she had not known what she had done.

"I did? I don't remember." She moved away from him, her arms wrapping around herself. "What did I do?"

Shea shook his head. "Ryanne, you are worrying me. Did you not realize you opened the door for me?"

Ryanne stared at him. "No, I didn't." Horror covered her face. "Shea! I could have let anyone in!"

"I know, love. I know." Shea rubbed at his face, his eyes on her, not quite sure how to proceed. "We have to do something, love. We can't have you opening the door to just anyone."

She nodded. "I know, but I don't know how. I'm scared, Shea. More scared than I have ever been."

He reached to pull her into his arms, his chin resting on her head. "What do we do? You need your independence."

"I do, but at what cost? Maybe I should have just moved home." She stared towards the wall before she was out of his arms and pulling down a photo. "This is not mine. I did not put that there."

A grim look on his face, Shea reached for Ryanne, pulling her to the door, scooping up her purse and shoes and slamming the door behind him. He propelled her swiftly across the parking lot and into his truck, despite her protests that she didn't have her shoes on. He reached for her feet, slipping on her sneakers, and then handing her the purse.

"Call Redmond or whoever of your family you want her. I'm putting in a call to the detective." He watched her face, seeing the fear turning to anger. "Anger won't help, love. Let's make our calls and then we talk."

"Talk? About what?" She stared at him, catching the look on his face he no longer tried to hide. "Shea?"

Shea simply shook his head and raised his phone, turning and walking a few feet away as he spoke with the detective, turning back to find Ryanne staring at him, her phone on the seat beside her. He sighed. Unknown to her family, they had been dating, seeing where it was heading. He knew he couldn't walk away from her, not ever. He just wasn't sure how she felt and if it was fair to her to be dating, going through what she was.

"Shea?" Ryanne had slipped from the truck and approached him, walking into his hug.

"He'll be here soon, love. He's sending a patrol officer in the meantime." He looked around, sensing someone near them. "We need to get you back into the truck and the doors locked. You're not safe out here."

She nodded. "I can't call them, Shea. I just can't."

"They're your family, love. They will want to know." He stood, truck door open, waiting for her to step up into it. "Ryanne? In the truck. Please."

She stared at him and then spun in a circle. "Someone's out here, Shea. I can feel them." She screamed his name as he was tackled and taken down, her own arms trapped against her body with what felt like a band of steel. Her phone flew from her hand as she struggled to escape, fear and panic rising within her.

Shea was dragged to his feet and arm twisted behind him, shoved towards a car. He struggled, pain showing on his face, as he tried to free himself and get to Ryanne. Shoved into the back seat of a car, he watched in horror as Ryanne was shoved into another vehicle. He reached for the door handle, his arm falling limp to his knee as a blow was struck across it before his wrists were bound roughly and a blindfold slapped across his face. He still struggled, trying to escape, trying to listen to the sounds of the traffic around them, struggling that was until he felt the prick of a knife through his sweatshirt and he froze in place, knowing he needed to remain unharmed, that he needed to be that way until he found Ryanne and they could escape.

Ryanne has struggled to get away, her feet kicking at her captor, her hands shoving at his arms, her head going back in a desperate attempt to hit him in the face, to no avail. She was carried bodily across to the other car and shoved inside, prevented from escaping through the other door by a tall thin man who was already seated on the back seat. She spun on the seat, her feet up to shove against her assailant when she froze, staring at the gun pointed directly at her face.

"Enough, Miss Stuart. Enough. If you don't stop, your boyfriend dies." The voice sounded familiar to her, but she just wasn't sure if she knew who it was.

She shook her head, trying to see past him, to find Shea but not seeing him. She slumped back against the seat, jumping in alarm as a cloth was bound over her eyes and then she heard the click of handcuffs around her wrists. Lord, she prayed, please. Let Shea get away. Protect him. I can't handle it if something happens to him. She didn't know any more if God even heard her. Lately, it didn't seem that He did.

She tilted her head, trying to hear the soft conversation, to understand what was being said but the words were too low. She tried to concentrate on the movement of the car, to count the stops, the turns but it was too confusing. She felt like they were driving around in circles. She felt the car finally stop and struggled against the hands that yanked her from the car and shoved her forward, her feet tangling and sending her to her hands and knees, the jar from the fall driving the breath from her. She cringed away from the heavy hand that pulled her to her feet and then propelled her forward, up some stairs and then through a building to land in a room, she thought, her handcuffs removed but with a caution to leave on the blindfold or face the consequences.

She listened to the stumbling feet that moved past her room and then heard a door slam in the distance, knowing that they had separated her from Shea. She crumpled even more to the floor, despair uppermost in her emotions.

Chapter 18

Two hours later, Redmond stood just outside the door to Ryanne's apartment, worry on his face as he watched the officers searching inside before he turned to study the parking lot, seeing the activity around Shea's truck. Where are you two, he asked silently?

Riordan walked towards him, Rory and Reilly beside him, Regan running to catch up. Redmond moved to meet them in the middle of the parking lot, his eyes searching before he looked at his father.

"Where's Mom?"

"She's on her way. She stopped to call the pastor and get the prayer line working." Riordan squinted against the sinking sun, the brilliant pinks and purples stopping him for a moment. "What do you know?"

"Not a lot, Dad." Redmond turned to face the building. "Apparently, Ryanne found another photo on the wall, Shea moved her out and to his truck. He had called in the detective, who sent a patrol officer. It doesn't look like he had time to get here before they disappeared."

"Any evidence that you've been told about?"

Redmond shook his head. "The detective said it's early yet to know if they've found anything. He wants us to go back through her apartment, to see if we notice anything odd or off."

"And do you think we will?" Regan moved restlessly, wanting to head out to find her sister but she had no real idea of where to search.

Riordan's attention was drawn to the officer heading their way and walked towards him. A few quiet words and Riordan moved towards the apartment, Redmond following closely, with his siblings hesitating before they too walked that way. Riordan stood for a moment in the doorway, his eyes searching for his daughter, not seeing her and not seeing Shea. He heard Redmond beside him, asking quiet questions that drew no answer or explanation.

Regan walked through the apartment, a frown on her face before she stopped beside Reilly.

"Where is she, Reilly?"

He shrugged. "They don't seem to have any idea. I wish I did." He peeked around her at Rory. "Rory, have you any idea?"

Rory didn't respond for a moment before he walked over to them, a photo in his hand. "Do either one of you know who this is?"

Regan and Reilly both shook their heads as they studied the photo.

"That's not one of hers. Nor one Shea has given her. Who is that?" Regan stared at it, a memory tickling at the edge of her mind before she shook her head, not quite sure what it was she was thinking.

Riordan reached for it, a sigh drawn from him. "I know him. He's the uncle of the girl who disappeared. What I don't understand is why it's here. Who put it in here?" He spun to study the door. "Didn't we set up a security system for her?"

"We tried. The landlord apparently refused. I didn't know until after Ryanne had moved in." Reilly paced, his face thoughtful. "Is the landlord working with that man?"

"That's a very good question, Reilly. We need to talk with him. Redmond, you're with me. Rory, Reilly, Regan, see what else you can find."

A week passed. Then, a second week. They found no signs of the couple. No ransom demand had arrived. Riordan had taken to pacing the house at night, Naomi worried about him as well as their daughter. Prayers rose steadfastly without an answer.

A few days later, Redmond ran for his car, his phone to his ear, searching for his father in the parking lot of their business and not seeing him. He tossed his phone to the passenger's seat as he keyed the motor to life and took off, dust swirling behind him. He had received a call that they may have found his sister and wanted him there. But, and there was always a but, the authorities were not sure they had the right house. A tip had come in but the person giving it had proven unreliable in the past.

He slammed on the brakes of his car and was out of it almost before he had it turned off, running towards his friend who stood waiting.

"Patrick? Do you have her?" Hope was in Redmond's voice and on his face, yet he tried to restrain it, knowing this might not be true.

"We have a good idea of where she is. This time, the tip was reliable." A hand to Redmond's arm drew him aside. "Our ETF officers are going in first."

"ETF? That doesn't sound good." Redmond shook for a moment, fear for his sister uppermost in his mind.

"It's standard, Redmond. I think I've explained that before. We send them in, they clear the building, and then we move in, paramedics with us."

Redmond paced as he waiting, pulling out his phone to call his father, then shoving it away again. He refused to raise their hope, not until he knew for sure Ryanne was found. Shea, too. He finally stood, hands jammed into his jacket pocket, collar turned up against the damp wind. He watched the activity going on around him, then watched as his friend, Patrick, moved towards the building, house, whatever you wanted to call it, he thought. Lord, I'm trusting. Please, dear Lord?

He raised his head from where he had been studying the ground as he felt a hand touch his shoulder. Patrick stood there.

"Patrick? What news?" Redmond was almost afraid to speak.

Patrick's hand tightened for a moment before he spoke, emotions overcoming him for a moment. "The paramedics have her, Redmond. They'll stabilize her and then bring her out."

"She's alive?" Redmond's knees buckled for a moment before he stiffened them and stood straight, his eyes flickering between his friend and the building.

"She's battered, Redmond. I can't lie about that. How bad, the paramedics are not saying."

"Shea?"

Patrick nodded, even as his attention drifted to a man standing near the police tape. He motioned to an officer, who moved that way, the man turning and walking rapidly away.

Patrick's attention went back to his friend, seeing how agitated Redmond had become. "Let me have your keys, Redmond. I'll have someone drive you to the hospital. They won't let you in there and they have said you can't ride with either one." He beckoned to an officer who ran towards them, hand out for the keys. "Here, Dennis will get you there. Call your folks. Do you have the contact information for Shea's people?"

"I do.   She's alive, Patrick?" Redmond knew he was repeating himself.

"She is. Head off now with Dennis."

Chapter 19

The door to the Emergency Department sliding open in front of them, Riordan and Naomi almost ran through it, her hand tight in his, searching for Redmond, finding him walking rapidly towards them, his arms out to hug them.

"Redmond? What word?" Riordan searched his son's face and then looked around, not seeing the rest of the family.

"She's not here yet, Dad. Patrick made me head here to wait. I've called the others. They'll be here as soon as they can. I also called Shea's people. They're out of town but will be here as soon as they can."

Riordan drew them aside and found seats for them, seating so he could watch the doors to the exam rooms, knowing they would come find Ryanne's family as soon as they could.

Redmond rose suddenly and walked towards Samuel and Shannon as they stood

139

inside the door, not sure where they should be heading.

"Redmond?" Shannon reached to hug her son's friend. "Any word?"

Redmond shook his head. "Not yet. All I know is that they were alive and the police and paramedics had them in their care. Over here. Mom and Dad are there."

Two hours later, Riordan rose, pacing, turning finally to face where Naomi and Shannon sat, quiet conversation between the two women. He watched as Redmond and Samuel spoke before his eyes rose to his other three children and their spouses. He frowned as he watched Leah rub at her abdomen. Their first grandchild was on its way and he worried that the stress from Ryanne's problems would affect Leah, even though she had laughing told him the doctor assured Rory and her that the baby was healthy.

He turned as he felt a hand touch his arm. The emergency physician stood there, watching the family before he drew Riordan to one side.

"Julian?"   Riordan's voice finally broke the silence as he studied his long-time friend, Julian Dempsey.

"Riordan?   She's alive and battered some, but not what I would have expected. She's been awake, not saying much, other than asking for Shea. She became agitated enough when we said he couldn't come to her that we've had to sedate her."

Riordan nodded, his mouth open to speak when Redmond spoke.

"They have a connection, Julian.   I have never seen it before. He's the only one who can calm her enough that we can deal with whatever we have to. How is Shea?"

"He's more battered that she is. From what he said, that happened to keep her in line and make her do what they wanted." Julian shook his head. "What is it with your family, Riordan? None of them so far, other than Redmond, have been able to stay out of trouble."

"When can we see them?"   Naomi spoke from beside Riordan, the rest of their family and Shea's family standing nearby.

"We've moved them to a ward, just getting them settled. Head up to the third floor. They'll be waiting for you to take you to them." Julian paused, a frown settling on his face as he watched Samuel, not quite sure where he knew him from. "They are under police guard at the moment."

A day later, Ryanne paced her family's living room, not happy with being there, but knowing she didn't want to go to her own apartment. Redmond sighed as he watched her, not sure how to even help her anymore. She was withdrawing from them, part of what she had gone through driving that. The other part, he just wasn't sure of. He turned to answer a question from Naomi and when he turned back, Ryanne was gone. He heard the softly closing door and ran for it, pulling it open but not seeing her.

"Ryanne? Where are you?" He walked towards her where she was leaning against his car. "What are you doing?"

She glared at him, her eyes shadowed. "You're doing it again, Redmond. Taking over."

He slumped beside her, even as he wrapped an arm around her. "I'm sorry.

No, I'm not taking over.   I'm just so worried.   I thought we had lost you for good."

She leaned against him. "I know. It was horrible, Redmond.   I didn't realize what the others had gone through. I want this over. Yesterday."

He laughed at the disgruntled tone in her voice. "Just trust God, Ryanne. I know you're struggling with that.   We all have been in some way, shape or form."   He waited, not saying anything. "What do you want to do? Your apartment?"

"I can't go back there.   And I can't find another. Whoever it is just finds me. I don't know where I'll live."

"We know that, hon.   Mom and Dad want you here, but I know that's not what you want." He held up a hand as she looked at him, stunned. "I'm not talking for you. I am not making plans. This is your life. You need to do this."

She sighed, knowing that whatever words Shea had used all those days ago had resonated with her oldest brother in a way no one else's would have. "Can I stay with you for a bit?"

He hugged her tighter. "That you can. I am glad to have you." He turned his head a bit, studying the house behind him. "How be we escape and I take you to see "him"?"

She groaned. "You'll never let me forget that, will you?"

He hugged her tighter to him. "If it really bothers you, I'll stop. But Shea has reached something in you that no one ever has. I don't know where it's going with you two, but I pray he stays in your life. You're different than you were, freer, happier. I like that in my little sister."

"Can we go find Shea? He called this morning, but I missed it. I need to make sure he's okay. It's my fault he was hurt."

"He'll never look at it that way, hon. I can promise you that much."

Two hours later, Redmond stood in the living room doorway at Shea's, hearing Shannon and Samuel talking quietly in the kitchen, before his eyes found his sister. She had curled up tight to Shea on the couch, who sat, legs stretched out in front of him.

He could see the quick grins and smiles coming and going on their faces as they talked quietly. He frowned as he noticed Shea's hand resting on Ryanne's legs where she had sat herself beside him, her own hand on his. He frowned even deeper as he watched her other hand rest on his shoulder, her chin on it. Then he sighed. She was content and happy, he thought. Lord, I have no idea where they're heading, but You do. He watched in disbelief as Shea's face turned to Ryanne, his free hand reaching to gently tug at one of her curls before he let it wrap around his finger, before he kissed her.

He jumped slightly as he felt an arm come around him and turn him away, drawing him to the kitchen. Shannon watched with compassion as he tried to compose himself before she shoved him into a chair, sitting beside him and reaching for his hands, a prayer rising from her lips for him.

"You didn't know?"

"Know that they were this close?" Redmond shook his head. "No. I don't know that any of us did."

"I think what they just went through changed something with them." Samuel slid a cup of coffee in front of Redmond before he too sat, his eyes on the doorway before he looked at Redmond. "Shea talked to me last night. I can't say what the conversation was about. That's confidential, but I know he deeply cares for your sister and has for a while."

Chapter 20

Standing in line at the bank, Shea's thoughts were not on the financial transaction he was there to make. Instead, his thoughts turned to his friend. Redmond had been quiet when he and Ryanne had left, not joking around like he usually did with Shea. Ryanne had stared at him with a puzzled look before she shrugged, her eyes searching Shea's face, asking without words if he knew what was going on.

Redmond had not called him either, which was so unusual, Shea thought. He moved forward with the line, knowing he would have to find his friend that day and work through what was going on. He turned finally, his thoughts clouded as he walked from the bank, knowing he needed to speak with his friend, but wanting to talk with Ryanne first. He headed for his truck, his footsteps slowing as he saw Riordan leaning against it. He sighed. Lord, he's not the one I want to talk to but it looks as if that's what You've planned.

Riordan watched as Shea headed towards him, a small smile on his face. He knew something was going on with his youngest daughter and Shea but hadn't asked. He knew he could but he wouldn't. He had to let Ryanne talk to him first. Or Shea, whichever one it would be.

"Shea? Do you have time for coffee?"

"I do."   He looked around.   "There. That cafe is good, isn't it?"

"It is."

Shea slid into a booth, watching as Riordan sat across from him, a folder laid on the table beside him. "You wanted to talk to me?"

"I did, Shea.   This has me puzzled, what you two went through. It's not making a lot of sense, is it? I mean, we haven't been told yet why you two.   Why you were taken."

Shea shook his head.   "I agree.   It doesn't make a lot of sense. Those photos she's been finding? Someone has dummied them up as if I did them, but I didn't. They're not what I do."

"That's true and it is puzzling. They have to be watching both of you closely. I don't like that."

"Nor do I. I don't want to see Ryanne hurt any more than she has been." Shea's glance dropped to the mug in front of him and the piece of lemon pie he had ordered. He shoved it away, until Riordan's hand stopped him.

"Eat your pie, Shea. We can talk, but we also need to make sure we eat." Riordan sipped at his coffee, not quite sure how to proceed.

"You wanted to talk, Riordan. What about?"

"This whole thing. It's not making a whole lot of sense, if you follow me."

"No, it's not. It all goes back to that woman who approached you two." Shea paused, a thought crossing his mind. "Did you find out anything more about her?" When Riordan shook his head, Shea hesitated before he spoke again. "What if she was that friend of Ryanne's who disappeared? Have you investigated that?"

Riordan stared at him for a moment before he shook his head. "I need you to come work for me. I don't know that we ever did just that. You may be on to something there."

Shea shrugged. "It all seems to be coming back to them. I don't want to see Ryanne hurt any more than she has been. She won't tell you, but she is struggling. She doesn't want to bother you or her family with her struggles and is hiding them from you."

"And she's confided in you."

Shea shook his head. "No, not really. It's just what she isn't saying that stands out."

Riordan shook his head once more. "How do you do that? How do you read her that well?"

Shea didn't respond, staring at the window behind Riordan before he spoke. "I don't know. It's just there."

Riordan finally rose, shoving the folder towards Shea. "Take a look at this. I found something interesting when I was doing some research this morning. I had no idea you would be at the bank this morning. Call me when you can." He walked away, leaving Shea staring after him, before he looked down at the folder.

Shea sat for a moment before he dropped money on the tabletop and then gathered the folder and walked from the cafe. He had no idea what Riordan had given him but he knew he needed to pray about it before he opened it.

Later that evening, Shea finally reached for the folder, hesitating for a moment, before he opened it, staring down at the top photo. Quietly, he flipped from photo to photo. They were not his, he knew that, but they showed him in all of them, Ryanne in some as well. He sighed. Who did this, Lord? How do we find them?

He reached for his phone as it chimed, a softened look on his face. Ryanne. How did she know he needed to talk to her right then?

He set his phone down carefully when he had finished his call, his eyes thoughtful before he rose and headed for his jacket. He needed to find Ryanne and talk to her in person. She was running, he knew, and he prayed she'd run to him.

Chapter 21

Ryanne shivered, wrapping her arms around herself. She knew Shea was on his way, but she wasn't sure he would be in time. She could feel evil around her. She sighed. Lord, she prayed, keep us safe. I didn't want to go through what the others did, but it seems there are other plans than mine.

Her mind drifted back, back to that day when Shea had rushed her away from her apartment to his truck. She shivered even now as she felt the evil that had approached them so quickly, the panic as she and Shea were separated. She had fought and fought hard to escape the arms around her waist, her feet kicking, her hands shoving at the arms, her nails scratching, her head hitting back against the face behind her.

Her mind turned back to the room she had been shoved into. It was damp, dark, paint peeling from the ceiling. She finally pulled the blindfold from her eyes, searching the room. She rose, tried the door and then the windows. She couldn't get out. Her heart sank. Now what, Lord? Where do I go from here? What do I do?

The day and night dragged by. She dozed, not ready to completely relax, not sure of what was coming. The dawn brought one of the men back to her door, dragging her to her feet and shoving her roughly towards the kitchen.

"Cook." The command was given in a guttural voice, as if he was trying to disguise it.

She stood, dumbfounded, shaking her head. "No. I won't cook."

Despite the many times she was ordered to do just that, she refused until her arm was roughly grabbed and she was spun around, only keeping her balance with the hand on her arm. She froze, a cry driven deep within her that she could not vocalize. Shea was shoved against a wall opposite her, a hand on his chest keeping him there, a knife to his throat. The steadfast look he sent her helped to steady her and give her the strength she needed to find.

"Cook, or he dies."

Shaking enough that she found it difficult to handle the pots and food, she desperately rushed to cook, not willing that Shea would be hurt because of her refusal to do just that. Meal after meal was the same. Shea would be threatened until she did what they asked. She couldn't eat. She had tried and the food had choked her. She didn't know if Shea was eating. She wasn't allowed to look at him, not since that initial time. She prayed for strength for them both, that Shea would be released, that someone would find them.

She didn't know to later that Shea paced his room as well, searching hourly for a way out and not finding it. His prayers soared through the dirty ceiling to heaven, asking for protection for the lady he loved, for escape for her, for release for the both of them. He feared for her life, not knowing who the men were. He frowned at one point, realizing nothing had ever been said about why they had been taken. He found that very strange.

She paced her room night and day, not willing to sleep, but knowing she needed to do that. She prayed constantly for release, for Shea's safety, for him to get away unharmed. She finally sank to the rough bed, pulling the blanket over her and sleeping.

She roused slightly the next morning, in the early hours, as she heard hurried footsteps and hushed voices, and then drifted back to sleep. She didn't hear the slamming of the doors as the men fled, gathering up what they could and leaving only clothing behind them.

She didn't hear the groans from Shea as he was battered back, prevented from reaching her, driven to the floor from the blows he took as he fought to reach her. She didn't rouse as the sun made its way across the sky, until early afternoon when activity outside the building drew the attention of the feral critters who slunk away, tails down, heads turned to watch the men over their shoulders, not sure if they had come for them or not.

Quiet rapid footsteps approached the rooms they were in. Neither one of them heard the exclamations given or the calls for the paramedics. Ryanne roused briefly, shaking her head at the men, asking for Shea. She gave what information she could before her eyes closed once more. She didn't feel her body lifted to the stretcher in gentle movements or the careful way it was moved to the ambulance. She didn't see the stretcher with Shea following to another waiting ambulance.

She had roused later that day, her eyes searching the hospital room before they slid closed and a tear trickled down her cheek. She had jumped as she felt a finger wipe it away and opened her eyes to find Rory watching her before he reached to hug her.

"Rory? Where am I?"

"You're safe, Ryanne. You're in the hospital. Shea is as well."

"He's okay?" She was almost afraid to ask. "They kept threatening him."

"He's bruised some. He said he fought to get to you this morning when the men were leaving."

"They just left?" She was astounded at the way that had happened. "God did that."

"He did, Ryanne." Rory watched as she drifted off to sleep, his arm around his wife as she stood beside him.

"She's hiding something, Rory."

"I know, Leah. I know. I just wish I knew what."

Chapter 22

Shea almost ran towards Ryanne as he watched her pacing near the lakeshore. He sighed, asking himself why she was there. Did she not know how much danger she was still it?   He thought of the photos in the truck, knowing he had to go over them with her. Something about them was just wrong. He needed to study them, but his first priority was Ryanne.

Ryanne turned as she heard soft footsteps in the sand and then ran to throw herself into Shea's arms. Her whole body was shaking and he couldn't get her to look up at him. He finally swept her into his arms and headed for his truck, tucking her inside, reaching behind her seat for a blanket to wrap around her. He slid behind the wheel, reaching for the heat button, turning it up high, his eyes on her.

"Ryanne? What happened?"

She jumped as she felt his hand on her arm before she turned to him. He drew in a deep breath at the look on her face and then took the phone she kept shoving towards him.

"Look at those, Shea! Who is doing this?"

He scrolled through the photos, his heart sinking as he realized they were the same as what Riordan had given him. "Your Dad gave me a copy of all of these. He didn't say where they came from." He glanced up at her, a grim look on his face. "We need to get this to your father." He keyed the motor to life and took off from the parking lot, a little quicker than was his normal speed, not seeing the car that followed them.

Ryanne watched as he stopped in front of a building. "Why here, Shea?"

"Because I am buying you a new phone with a new number." He poked a finger at the phone she still held. "You're not using that one anymore."

"But I need to."

"Not right now. We'll give the number to your family and my parents. No one else. That one stays active and you can access the voice mail from a landline."

She finally sank back, realizing just what he was saying. "You think someone found my number and is stalking me?"

He nodded. "That's exactly what I think." He reached to the back seat for the folder. "Here. Look through these while I'm inside. Tell me what you see in them."

She sat, her hands on the folder, her eyes on the store door, not willing to look at the photos, knowing she should but fear welled up inside her. She couldn't do that, noting Shea stood where he could watch his truck through the front window of the store as he waited for the clerk to finish the transaction. He quickly moved back to his truck, the new phone extended to her. She stared at it and then up at him, a frown on her face as she studied him, before she sighed and reached for it.

"Do you really think this is necessary?"

"I do. We need to keep you safe and I can't think of any other way than this." He stared through the windshield, not quite sure where he stood with her, even though they had been considering themselves a couple for the last month or so. "Ryanne? Can I ask you something?"

"That sounds ominous. Why would ask that and not just ask your question?" She smiled as his head flipped around and he stared at her before his mouth clamped closed.

He shook his head even as he reached for her hand, bowing it to pray for them before he spoke. "Where do we stand, Ryanne? I mean, you and I, as a couple? I know where I would like it to be, but I'm not sure you're ready for that."

She sighed, her gaze out the side window as she thought through his question. "I am not sure, Shea. I know where I'd like us to be, but with what's going on, I don't think it's fair to you." She looked over at him as he tugged on her hand. "What? Now what do you want?"

"Nothing, except to reassure you that I will do everything I can to keep you safe." He backed out of his parking spot. "We need to talk to your Dad."

"I know." Shea laughed at the disgruntled sound in her voice. "It's just that he'll want to take over and wrap me in bubble wrap or something like that."

"I would, too, my love." He pulled to the side of the road, a frown on his face as he watched in his rearview mirror. "We have company, Ryanne, and I don't think it's good company. Hold on."

She shot a look behind her, fear coursing through her. "It's them, isn't it? They've found us."

"They have but hold on. I'll try and lose them, if I can." Shea suddenly spun his wheel, accelerating and heading back the way he had just come, watching as the car behind him spun out and hit the curb. He spun his wheel again and headed away from that area, towards the building where he knew he would find his father.

"You're not heading for my parents?"

He shook his head. "No. I'll try Dad. They'll be looking for you with your family. Maybe we can throw them off this way."

Samuel watched as Shea paced the kitchen, his eyes worried for a moment before they turned to watch Ryanne, finding her sitting, calmly he thought until he caught the look in her eyes. She's terrified, isn't she, Lord? How do we reach her, give her Your reassurances when we don't have them ourselves?

He sat beside her for a moment, his eyes on his son, before he spoke.

"Ryanne, did you look through those photos?"

She shook her head. "Not the ones Dad gave Shea. I did on my phone." She frowned. "I don't know why they sent them to me."

"That's what's got me, Dad." Shea slid into a seat beside Ryanne, reaching for the folder and flipping it open. "Why send them to both Ryanne and Riordan? That doesn't make sense."

"No, on the surface, it doesn't. But it has to." He glanced between the two. "I understand it was a relative of your friend that was in the picture found in your apartment?"

She nodded. "So, I'm told. I don't remember him at all." She looked up at the ceiling, blinking back tears, angry with herself that she was letting her emotions get the better of her. "Why, Samuel? I didn't kill her. I tried to help. I tried to find her. I ended up in the hospital myself because of that."

"We understand. But there has to be something else there, something you've forgotten."

She shook her head, her eyes on Samuel. "There isn't. I mean, we were friends but not that close. We did things in a group, never on our own."

"We're looking into that, both Shannon and myself as well as your family. So far, we haven't found anything, but there is something there. I know that. We just haven't trace it back yet. Not quite. We have a few leads that we're tracking down. Regan is like a bulldog with that."

Ryanne began to laugh, causing the two men to stare at her. "You've described her so well. That's exactly how she is when it's someone close to her. She did that with Rory and Reilly. We did that for her when she finally let us." She paled and then buried her head in her arms.

Shea and his father exchanged a glance before Shea's arm was around her. "Ryanne? What it is?"

"I think there's more to it than Mary. I think it's related somehow to Dad and I don't know how." She raised her face and they were taken aback by the devastation on her face.

Chapter 23

Rory stared at Redmond as he stood in front of him, head shaking, hands waving even as his mouth opened and closed. He could hear Reilly and Regan bickering behind him somewhere and could see his parents deep in conversation with Shea's parents. He knew Leah, Aideen and Delaney were somewhere about as were Ryanne and Shea. Just where that couple was, he wasn't quite sure. All he knew was that his father had called a family meeting and every one of them had turned up. It was just that the meeting had not happened yet, and everyone was on edge.

Ryanne was suddenly in the midst of them, a furious look on her face. She spun and stared at each one before she was running from the room. Rory saw the tears on her face and ran after her but wasn't quite quick enough to stop her running for the door and through it. He followed, not seeing her, but seeing Shea heading for the garden at the back, waving as he did so. Rory followed, not quite sure what he would find.

Ryanne slid to a stop near the centre garden and wrapped her arms around herself, not heeding Shea's calls to her. He stopped away from her, watching closely, knowing she needed space from them. Rory went to move around him but Shea's hand on his arm stopped him and he shot him a questioning look.

"Wait, Rory. Just wait. She needs some time. She's fine with us here, just doesn't want us close to her." Shea looked around, feeling a sense of being watching and of impending doom. "She's trying to stand on her own two feet and isn't sure how to do that, not quite yet."

Ryanne moved in a circle, her eyes on the edge of the property, feeling someone out there, just not sure who. She turned back to face Shea and Rory, not quite sure either now to approach them. Well, how to approach Rory. Shea and she had come to an agreement the night before and she glanced down at her hand where his ring sparkled in the sunshine. She was content with that, happy in her new love, knowing

God had prepared them for each other. It was her brother she didn't know how to approach. Rory being out there? He was at risk, and she hated that for him.

A scream rose in her throat as she felt an arm come around her and trap her own arms against her body, the scream dying in her throat as a heavy hand clamped itself across her mouth. She struggled to escape, watching in horror as first Rory and then Shea were taken to the ground. Rory lay motionless. Shea struggled before he was pulled roughly to his feet, hands bound behind him and shoved forward, stumbling over his feet, falling to his knees at one point before he was yanked up and once more shoved forward.

Ryanne was shoved roughly after him, her hands bound now in front of her, a gag tied across her moth. She could hear commotion behind her and knew that Rory was on his feet and coming behind her.

She fought against the hand holding her, desperate to escape, to find a way for the two men to get away. She struggled against being shoved into a vehicle and to the floor, where a heavy foot landed on her back to keep her still. She heard the commotion as the two men were shoved inside and then silence. Her heart sank. Lord? Why? You promised protection. This does not feel much like it.

The three captives felt the vehicle move away and knew that at the moment there was no chance they could get away. Prayers rose from them all, each different, but having the common theme of pleading for safety and escape.

Riordan was on a search, his two sons and Samuel with him. He needed to talk to Ryanne but could not find her anywhere. He stood, hand on the top of his head, staring around the house before he ran for the door, yanking it open and having it slam against the wall with the force of his pull. He ran for the yard, searching, not seeing them, and his heart sank. Where were they?

Reilly ran for the security room, hoping to find out what had happened to his sister. He knew that wherever she was the other two were there more than likely. His heart sank as he saw them capture and subsequent removal of them. He felt a hand on his shoulder and reached to wrap an arm around Aideen as she sank to the chair arm.

"They're gone?"

He nodded grimly. "They are. Rory was hurt, I think. So far it looks as if Ryanne and Shea are not harmed." He glanced around as he heard footsteps and Leah appeared in the doorway.

"Reilly? He's gone?" Fear briefly flickered across her face.

"He is. I'm sorry, Leah."

"It's not your fault. You didn't know. God will protect them and bring them back to us." She spun and walked away, her steps hurried on the hardwood floor.

Reilly gave a sound and went to rise, prevented by the pressure of Aideen's arm around his neck, and looked up at her, finding her watching the still photos he had drawn up.

"Aideen?"

"How did they get past your security, Reilly? How? It's too good. An alarm should have sounded."

"That's what puzzling me." He was on his feet, Aideen's hand in his, as he ran for the outside and then towards his father.

"Reilly?" Riordan had been watching for him.

"They've been taken. All three. Rory was down and looks as if he was hurt, but Ryanne and Shea are fine. The thing is, someone got into here without sounding the security alarm. And I know it was on. I tested it first thing this morning, knowing Ryanne would be here."

Riordan paled. "Someone sold us out, is that what you're saying?"

Reilly shook his head. "Not sure, Dad. But somehow they managed to circumvent our system. They were taken out the back. Likely the kidnappers had a vehicle waiting." He rubbed at his face, his eyes on Samuel. "I just don't get what they want."

"That is a puzzle, Reilly, one we need to solve." Samuel watched Redmond for a moment before he spoke again. "Where can we work? I need to pull up some software and search. This seems familiar. I've seen this in the past. I just need to verify some facts."

Riordan stared at him for a moment and then pointed towards the house. "Reilly, show Samuel where he can work. Redmond, we're searching. If I can keep the police out of this for now I will." He waved his hand at a protest rising from the three with him. "I will call them in an hour. I promise."

"It's too late, Dad. Mom already called." Redmond had standing facing the house and saw his mother walking towards them.

"She didn't, did she?" Riordan finally turned to face Naomi.

"I did. No more, Riordan. We have to involve the police. I asked for the detective who was assigned to Ryanne's case to come. He is on his way."

Two weeks had passed, with no ransom demand, no sign of the three who were missing. Riordan worried about Rory's wife, Leah, knowing she trying not to show how worried she was and yet concerned about the baby she was carrying. They were all trying, he thought, to be positive, to search, but he felt they were trying too hard. He had finally sent Regan and Delaney home. Leah, he had wanted to keep with them but she had insisted she needed to go back to her bed and breakfast. She could worry and pray just fine there, she informed them as she walked away.

Naomi was not sleeping, he knew, hearing her pace the house during the early morning hours and he would arise, find her and then spend time in prayer. He searched daily, trying to find them, but not.

He had no further idea how the men had managed to get in without the alarm sounding. Reilly had searched the system and found a blip in it, just long enough for the kidnapping to have happened. He was trying even then to trace back the issue but was not able to. They both suspected one of their employees but couldn't place blame without knowing for sure.

Samuel had been around, in and out over the weeks, desperately trying to find a clue, a hint of where they might be. He had researched deeply into Mary and her family and was finding that she and they were not who they had led everyone to believe. Riordan had stared at him when he first presented evidence of illegal activities and shook his head but held out a hand for the thick folder Samuel kept shoving at him. He glanced through it, his face paling even as he read a paragraph here and there, saw the documentation going back beyond Mary's parents.

Reilly tracked him down one day, flopping down in the chair in front of him, his head dropping back to rest against the high back of the chair.

"Reilly?" Riordan was concerned about his family, but particularly Reilly. He was bearing the brunt of guilt, that his father knew.

"Dad, I just don't get it. Where are they?"

"I wish I knew, son. I'd go in and get them." He sat back, his pen tapping on the desk, until he frowned and dropped it. That wasn't helping out anything, he decided. "Samuel has certainly pulled up information for us that I never expected."

"And so has Abe Finlay and his wife, Emma. She is working relentlessly to try and help but even she is hitting roadblocks." He sighed even as he pulled out his phone to check an email that had just arrived. "Emma just sent an email. She's found some names and is working through them. I want this over, Dad."

"We all do. I just don't understand." He looked up as Redmond hesitated in the doorway. "Redmond?"

"I'm sorry, Dad. I thought she was safe." Redmond blinked back his emotions. This was his little sister that was missing. He remembered his father placing her into his arms when he was six or so and she was a newborn. He had looked down at her, feeling her fingers curl around his finger, and then looked up at his father, promising to protect her with every fibre of his being. He felt like a failure, that he had been unable to do just that. It had been different with Regan. They were closer in age and she was more independent. Ryanne just seemed to need her older brother, although she had been vocal as a toddler that she could do it all on her own.

Riordan sighed and rose, his arms drawing his oldest son into a hug, and feeling the tears Redmond could not hold back. Reilly watched, compassion on his face as his brother struggled with his emotions, and then looked back down at his phone, excusing himself to take a call, turning to watch his father and brother.

"Redmond, sit, son." Riordan drew him down on the black leather couch near the desk, his arm around his son's shoulders. "You could not have prevented this. If you had been there instead of Rory, you would have disappeared. God knows you are needed here, to help search. We need your expertise in that. Rory will help to keep Ryanne safe, as well Shea."

"Shea! What did I do, Dad, when I involved him?"

Riordan gave a low laugh. "I don't think you involved him. I think he involved himself." He stared across the room, biting at his lip for a moment, not sure if he should say anything. "Shea talked to me a few days before they disappeared."

"He did? About what?" Redmond's head was turned to watch his father. "No, they didn't, did they?"

"No, not married. Shea wants your sister to have all the fun and trappings that she wants. He asked for her hand and I agreed. He didn't have to do that. Ryanne is quite capable of making up her own mind, you know."

"I'm finding that out more and more." He sat back, his eyes on the window. "Dad, those photos? Did we ever track down all the people in them?"

"Paul is working on that. He's been in contact with that Emma and her staff. Names are slow to come in and that is concerning. Emma told him that is not how it usually is. They are having to dig through multiple aliases."

They both looked up as Reilly returned and slumped down into a chair across from them, his eyes on the floor, before he looked up.

"Reilly?"

"They found the van, Dad. Stripped and empty. The detective said they'll tow it in and look it over, but he really didn't expect to find much in it."

"We didn't think they would. And it would have been stolen. That's a given." Riordan looked up as Samuel appeared in the doorway and hesitated before entering. "Samuel?"

Samuel shook his head. "Nothing new. Not yet. I just wish I knew where they were." He too sat, his arms crossed over his chest. "Has anyone gone back over the photos?"

"Regan and Naomi were. I think Shannon was too. Why?"

"Because I have a feeling the clue to finding them is there. And we're missing it." He raised his head, staring at the ceiling, his heart praying for the three younger people. "I wish I had access to Shea's programs. They might help."

Reilly gave a sound and was on his feet, almost running from the room, back in short order with a folder in his hands. "I had almost forgotten. Shea had given me a folder earlier that day. He asked if we could look at it. I set it aside and forgot about it." He flipped through it and then his hand froze, his eyes wide as he looked up at his father. "It's here, Dad. Shea found what we were missing." He handed over Shea's notes.

Riordan studied them and then was on his feet, running from the room, heading for a vehicle, the rest of the men behind him, leaving the women staring after them until Regan raced to follow, sliding into a seat almost too late.

Chapter 25

Riordan raised the binoculars to his eyes, searching along the low hills for an opening, a cave, anything where someone could be hidden.

"You're sure, Reilly?"

"I am, Dad. Shea was specific about this area. We know it well. There are caves here, but I don't see that there has been a lot of activity around."

"Not lately, although with the winds and waves, any trace could have been washed away." He handed the binoculars to Samuel. "Do you see anything?"

"No, I don't. We'll need to move in closer. I don't like doing that in daylight, though."

"Twilight would be best. Fall back, everyone. We need to make plans and retrieve the equipment we have. Regan? You'll need your medical supplies." Regan was a trained paramedic for their team.

They crept away, not seeing the man who had been hidden watching them, before he too rose and followed them. The man turned away once he saw they were leaving and faced the shore once more, before shaking his head and moving away. He had to find someone and send that person to Riordan. He could not go himself.

Reilly looked up as their secretary, Anna, paused in his office doorway, her head turned to watch the reception area before she entered and closed the door behind her.

"Anna? What is going on?"

She shook her head, a puzzled look on her face. "I have someone here, asking for you. I have never seen her before, but she insists she needs to speak with you. It's urgent."

Reilly stared at Anna for a moment before he rose and walked through to the reception area, studying the young woman who stood there. Around his age, he thought, taking in her height, the dark blond hair pulled back into a braid and the curious green eyes with the amber tint to them.

"Can I help you?"

She jumped as he spoke, spinning to stare at him even as he grinned. "If you are Reilly Stuart, then you can. Is there somewhere we can speak in private?"

Reilly shrugged, and then motioned towards the boardroom behind her. "In there, I think. Can I offer you a coffee or water or something?"

"Thank you, but I'm fine. This will not take long."

She sat in the chair he indicated, her hands rubbing along her legs. "This is hard. I was asked to come and find you, to give you information. The person who asked cannot do that himself."

"I see." Reilly leaned his arms on the table, his eyes intent on her. "Why not?"

"Because he's undercover, I think, and can't be seen in town." She sighed. "I wish he had found someone else. I don't do this."

Reilly began to laugh, drawing a frown from her.

"I'm sorry. You just sounded so definite there and so much like my sisters. First, can I get your name?"

"I'm sorry. I should have started with that. I'm Sloane Everett. My father and I run a backpacking/hiking company in the area. We're fairly new to this town. Anyway, I was approached, given an envelope, and asked to pass it on to you." She reached into her pack and pulled it out. "He said you'd find everything you needed in it." She rose, her eyes on him. "I can't stay and answer any more questions. I really don't know what's going on." She walked away from him, almost running into Redmond as she exited the room, whose hand came out to help her balance.

Redmond watched as she walked away, a frown on his face before he turned to find Reilly standing beside him, staring first at Sloane and then the envelope in his hand.

"What is that all about, Reilly?"

Reilly shrugged at the tone of curiosity in his brother's voice. "I really don't know. She said she was given this envelope and my name and asked to give it to me." He studied the envelope before he walked over to Anna's desk, taking the letter opener she was holding out for him. "I guess I have to open this, don't I?"

"It would help if you did, Reilly." Anna's face showed her worry. "Do you think it will help?"

He shrugged, even as he pulled out the folded papers. "I have no idea. Redmond, let's you and I look this over before we go to Dad."

Reilly sat back once he had handed the papers over to Redmond, watching his oldest brother closely before he spoke.

"Is this legit, do you think?"

Redmond shrugged as he flipped through the papers, pausing once in a while to re-read a portion. "Whoever this is has done good work. He seems to have been watching us earlier today when we were out there. I didn't see him. Did you?"

Reilly shook his head. "No, and that's concerning, isn't it?"

Chapter 26

Standing inside the deepest cave, Samuel looked around, not seeing evidence that the three had ever been there, before he turned to Riordan.

"What are your thoughts?"

Riordan shook his head. "I think they've been here, at some point, but it's difficult now to be sure. Whoever it was that sent the letter seemed sure they had been here."

"I would like to talk to him. Or at least to the young lady who brought that letter."

"I tried to reach her before we came out here. She's apparently away on a trip, left just after she spoke with Reilly. I can't confirm a date or time when she'll be back. They wouldn't give me that information, just said they'd have her call me."

"That's only fair." Samuel turned as Redmond approached. "What do you have, Redmond?"

"Rory's watch. It was in the next room. So, they were here but where are they now?"

"I have no idea. The watch is dry, so it can't have been too long." Redmond handed it off to his father, who stared at it before looking up, a bleak look around his eyes.

"It's stopped on today's date. He was here today. We missed him." He turned and strode from the room, leaving Redmond and Samuel sharing a look before they walked after him, seeing his phone in his hands.

"He'll be calling the detective." Samuel spoke quietly.

"I am sure he will be. This doesn't help us, does it?" Redmond was grasping for hope.

Samuel shrugged. "It tells us at least Rory was here and was likely alive. He may well have been the one to leave the watch." He motioned towards Riordan. "We need to pull away from here and let the police do their thing."

Naomi and Shannon watched as the five walked back towards them, ducking under the tape the police had strung, mouths opening and then closing without asking their questions.

Riordan silently handed Naomi Rory's watch and she clutched at it, hope springing up in her heart.

"They were here? He was right?"

"It appears that he was, sweetheart." Riordan's arms encircled Naomi. "I just don't know where they are now. They seem to have been moved." He nodded towards the activity, watching as a crowd of curious onlookers gathered. "Let's get out of here. I let the detective know he could find us at home. Samuel? Shannon?"

"Let's get our families out of here." Samuel drew Shannon with him. "Did anyone call Leah?"

"Aideen did, I think. She said Leah was content to stay where she was for now, that she could be here in short order when she was needed." Naomi spoke up.

Pacing the house, Riordan waited as the hours went by and still no word came. He had received a call earlier from the detective, who had apologized that he had

been called out to another case, but that he
would be in touch as soon as he could be.

Shea rolled his head, trying to stretch the neck muscles that had begun to cramp. He tugged at the cuffs binding his arms behind him and fastening him to a post. His head went back to rest against it even as his eyes slid shut. He had lost track of time, sleep being kept from them. His eyes burned as he opened them again, searching for Ryanne and then Rory. Ryanne was across the room from him. He watched as she struggled to sleep, her head resting on her upraised knees, her face buried from his sight. He twisted his head to watch Rory, concerned about his friend, not seeing much movement from him. Let him be okay, please, dear Lord? They have been rough on him, trying to bring Ryanne to terms. She just doesn't know what they want and they refuse to accept that.

He sighed, knowing that the men would be back in a few minutes. They always were. They rotated who was there, but there was two men who seemed to be in charge, taking turns to watch the abuse the three had undergone.

He thought back to the caves, where they had first been kept and had been allowed a certain amount of freedom. They had been moved from there so abruptly, Shea had had hope that they had been found, but instead, they were moved to a building outside of town. He knew that because of the quiet he could hear outside, the sounds of a forest dimly seeping through the cracks and crevices in the walls and ceilings.

He puzzled through what the men were asking from Ryanne. It had started off as a treasure box, but then had changed to something more sinister. They were now asking for papers and documents they said she had. She had denied having them, in tears at times. The tears brought swift retribution on them, usually directed at Rory, but now at him. He didn't know how long she would last. She was giving up, he could tell. He prayed for them all, particularly for Ryanne. He didn't know how much longer they would be kept, but he prayed they would be released soon.

He heard the heavy footsteps approaching and then the grating of the key as it turned in the old-fashioned lock. He ducked his head to avoid the shafts of bright light streaming through the door before it was slammed shut.

The men stood, eyeing each one, before they exchanged glances. This was it, they had decided. Either they learned what they wanted today or else they would walk away and leave the three here, to die without being discovered.

Ryanne raised her head as she heard the footsteps stop in front of her, blinking to clear her blurry eyes, not focusing on the men, but on Shea across from her. She read his signals of love and trust and belief in her and sighed. Why, Lord? Why me? What do I have that they want? I have nothing for them. I am completely drained.

She simply shook her head at the demands, not meeting the men's eyes. Her head was turned partially away from the leader when the blow was struck, slamming her face into the pole she was bound to. Intense pain lanced through her face even as she cried out and then crumpled into a heap as close to the floor as she could reach.

Shea's yells of protest resounded through the room, rousing Rory from his stupor to add his protests. Shea watched in horror as another blow was aimed at Ryanne, even as he struggled to escape and reach her. He didn't see the man approaching him from the side until a heavy boot was launched into his side and he felt his ribs crumple under the steel toe of the boot. He sank into darkness, his last thought a prayer for safety for his lady.

Rory stared in horror at first Ryanne and then Shea before he rasied his eyes to the man standing in front of him, who simply shook his head and then walked away, the door slamming shut behind them. He struggled to escape, rubbing his wrists raw from the metal cuffs, but not finding release. He slumped back, his eyes on his sister, not knowing how severely she was injured, just knowing he could not reach her.

His chin dropped to his chest. He puzzled through the demands of the men, trying to make sense of what they had asked, and then he sighed. It all came back to that Mary, he thought. She can't have been who she said she was. If that was the case, then who was she? Who were her parents, then? His eyes drifted closed as he prayed, and he slept, not a proper sleep but a sleep he might not wake up from.

None of them heard the creaking of the door late that night, or saw the filtered beams of the lights that were flashed through the room or the low cries of surprise and horror. They didn't feel the hands on them, or the call for bolt cutters to release them.

Rory roused, his head raising as he stared around before he sat up with help, his father's arm keeping him upright. He blinked at his father, not sure it was really him, convinced he was dreaming.

"Rory? Are you alright?" Riordan's voice was low in his ear.

"Not sure, Dad. Ryanne?" He peered around his father, to see Regan working on her sister. "How is she? They were really rough on her."

"We can see that. Let's get you up and on your feet." Riordan pulled his son to his feet, an arm around him to steady him. "Let's get you out of here. Shea and Ryanne will be right behind us."

Regan looked up at her father, a slight shake of her head. She was afraid for her sister. She could see the large purple bruising on her face and when she touched it gently, Ryanne had cried out in her unconscious state and jerked away from her touch. Reilly reached to gather gather her into her arms, standing and nodding to Regan.

Regan stood, moving towards where Shea was standing, unsteady on his feet, his father's arm around him even as he pulled Shea's arm over his own shoulder.

"Shea?" Regan's voice brought his attention to her.

"Ryanne? How is she?" Shea's voice was barely above a whisper.

"She's hurting, Shea. We need to get her looked at. Let me take a look at you." She reached to touch him, drawing back as he stepped away from her and then made his way slowly from the room, leaving his father staring after him.

"Samuel?" Regan's low voice filled with concern caught his attention.

"Regan, we need to get out of here now. There's nothing here." He caught at her arm and dragged her from the room, their feet pounding on the flooring as they ran for the exit. Hearing a sound of breaking timber, they slid to a stop, spinning to stare at the ramshackle building as it collapsed in on itself, before they shared a look of horror.

Riordan stood beside them, his arm around his oldest daughter, shock on his face. "Thank God you made it out."

"It was timed somehow, Riordan, to collapse. Whoever it is didn't want those three to make it out."

"No, they didn't. Let's move, people. Out of here. Regan, in with them until we can the team waiting for us." Riordan had made the call he hadn't wanted to but knew he had to. Teams of paramedics would be waiting down the road for them, waiting for the three they had just pulled from the building. He turned once more to study it. They would find no evidence now, he thought. Not in the building but maybe outside it.

Shea once more shook off helping hands as he stood, watching as Ryanne was gently placed on a stretcher, his hand coming out to touch her hair before he stood back, anger rising in him as he saw her face. He sighed. Anger wouldn't help. That much he knew, but it still burned within him. He moved, sudden pain driving him to his knees and then to the ground even as his vision darkened. He heard faint cries and then nothing.

Paramedics were there, assessing him, finding the ribs that had been damaged in the vicious kick. Samuel watched, horror on his face, as his son struggled to breathe. He knew what had happened. He had seen it before. A collapsed lung. He heard the faint murmurs of the men working over his son and then climbed hurriedly into the ambulance, refusing to leave even as the stretcher was loaded. An oxygen mask covered Shea's lower face even as Samuel reached to touch his son's hair.

"How bad?" His voice was quiet, too quiet, as he turned to the lead paramedic.

"Bad, Mr. Murdoch. Bad. His lung has collapsed."

"A rib, you're not saying."

The two men exchanged a glance, no words necessary. Samuel's vision turned to the ambulance speeding along behind him. He wasn't sure which Stuart sibling it held, but he could and would pray for both of them and for their families. And for his. He prayed that Leah would be there at the hospital, but knowing it was unlikely.

Chapter 28

Leah almost ran through the doors, her eyes searching for Rory or his family. Regan ran towards her, hugging her and then drawing her to where the families sat.

"Regan? What aren't you telling me?" Leah searched Regan's face.

"He's alive, Leah. They're working on assessing him but they don't think other than malnutrition and lack of sleep he's been harmed." Regan's voice died away even as her eyes caught her father's glance.

"But the others? Ryanne? Shea?" Leah's worried look moved among the all. "What aren't you saying about them?"

"Shea's being treated for a collapsed lung, I think they said. Isn't that correct, Samuel?" He nodded even as Regan continued to speak. "We don't know much more than that. I am not sure what all is wrong with Ryanne. They seem to have made her their special task."

Leah watched for a moment, then was on her feet, heading the clerk's desk, speaking to her for a moment and then heading through the doors to the exam room. She refused to wait, wanting and needing to see Rory. She stepped to once side as a stretcher approached, a hand going to her mouth as she saw Ryanne, praying as she had not prayed for a long time.

She finally stood at Rory's side, her hand on his arm, watching as his head shifted restlessly before her hand found his cheek and brought stillness to him. She refused to leave, even as the nurses worked around her. Naomi finally found her, an arm around her daughter-in-law, as she watched her son sleep.

"What have they said, Leah?"

"He's dehydrated. Fatigued. He has some bruising, but they don't think he was treated as badly as the others." She looked up, tears sparkling in her eyes. "Why, Naomi? Why them? What did they want?"

"I am not sure. None of us are. We haven't been able to talk to Ryanne or Shea yet. The physicians won't let us. In fact, we haven't even been able to see them yet."

"You haven't? That's not right!" Leah turned to leave, to go and find some to rectify that when Naomi's hand stopped her.

"It's okay, Leah. They are both in surgery."

"Surgery? No one told me that." Leah slumped back against the bed, her eyes on Naomi. "Why?"

"Shea has a collapsed lung and they have to deal with the broken ribs and put in a chest tube, I think they said." Naomi drew a deep breath even as she hesitated. "Ryanne? The surgeon said her jaw is broken in a couple of places. They weren't sure about any other fractures in the facial bones. He said she seems to have been slammed into something."

"Naomi! Who would do that?" Leah reached to hug the woman she had begun to think of as a mother.

"We don't know. The police are looking into it, but haven't gotten very far." Naomi began to pace, her eyes returning over and over to Rory, willing him to awaken, but knowing he needed to sleep.

She turned as she heard footsteps heading their way.

The nurse paused for a moment, her eyes on Leah and then moving to Rory. "Mrs. Stuart?"

"Leah, please. What can you tell me?" Leah drew in a deep breath, fearing the worst.

The nurse smiled. "It's okay. We're moving him to a room shortly. I just wanted to let you know." She glanced over at Naomi. "And we have not had word on the other two yet. Once we move Rory, how be you two head up to the surgical floor? Your family's already there."

"I'll wait with Leah, thank you. It's Brenna, isn't it?"

"That would be me. I'll be back shortly."

Samuel and Shannon finally stood at Shea's side, watching him closely. Samuel's glance took in the medical equipment around him even as he heard the beeps and whirrs from each piece. Shannon's hand rested against her son's face for a moment.

"Who, Samuel?"

"I wish I knew, love. I want them."

"I do, too. Will he be able to tell us, do you think?"

Samuel shrugged, feeling that that had been all he had been capable of lately. "I don't know. I pray he does. I want this over for him and Ryanne. She's been through enough."

"Any word?" Shannon turned to watch the door. "I'll be back. I'm going to find her family. Surely they've heard something."

Samuel watched her stride away, seeing the anger she was trying so hard to control, and knowing it matched his own. This was something God would have to deal with in them, taking away their anger and replacing it with peace.

Chapter 29

Riordan watched as the surgeon walked their way. It was late evening by then and he had begun to despair that they would have news shortly. He had sent the others to find food. Naomi, he knew, was with Rory.

"Gary?" He greeted a fellow church member, Gary Prentice.

"Riordan? I knew you would be here. Let's sit. It's been a long day and is far from over for me." Gary sank into a chair, his eyes closing briefly.

"Gary? What can you tell me?"

Gary sighed. "You need to find whoever did this. They are brutal. I just pray she's never in their hands again."

Riordan paled, even as he felt Naomi's arm slip around his. He reached for her hand, grasping it tightly, praying for his daughter. "Gary? What did they do?"

"Her jaw? Fractured in three places. We've wired it together. Thank God we could preserve her teeth. That took some work. She also has some hairline fractures in the cheek bone. They will heal on their own. It could have been much worse. I was worried about the orbital area." He looked up at that point. "Around her eye. There was bruising right up into her hairline. So far, there doesn't seem to be anything other than bruising. Her face is really swollen, so be prepared for that."

Naomi's face had paled at his words. "Her eye?"

"I've had the specialist in. It's fine so far, he said, but he will want to see her once the swelling goes down." He looked up as he heard himself paged through the hospital system. "I have to run. Another case is waiting for me. Ryanne's in recovery. Someone will come find you when she's moved to a room. I want her in ICU for a day or so." He paused once more. "Her friend?"

"Shea? He's in a room somewhere here."

Gary nodded. "I've been in to see him. He woke briefly, struggled to tell me he tried to get free to help her and couldn't. He's hurting, Riordan. Make sure all three get help." He stood and walked away, leaving the couple staring at one another.

"How's Rory?" Riordan wrapped his wife in his arms, needing that contact with her.

"He's sleeping now. They brought in a bed for Leah, worried about her being up."

"That's good." Riordan stared at the wall across from him. "What are we missing, Naomi? You're good at this. You like to solve these mysteries. What have we not found?"

"I'm wondering if it comes back to a dinosaur of some kind. Ryanne has to have seen or heard something for that to come out. It's not like her."

"That's what we think. We need to talk to her again, to see what she remembers. It appears to go back to that friend of hers, that Mary."

"I know. There was always something odd about that family, but we could never figure it out." Naomi's head went down on her husband's shoulder. "Has anyone ever been able to prove she's dead?"

Riordan froze. "You're looking at it wrong. We're trying to prove she's not dead."

Naomi's head moved against him as she shook it. "No, we need to prove she is dead, that she's not alive. If we can do that, then maybe we can find out who's behind this." Her voice died away as her breath softened and she slept.

Riordan stared at the wall, realizing that Naomi had just upturned their investigation. He wondered if this was what Emma had been up to. It would seem so, from what she had been sending him.

He looked up as he heard soft footsteps and the nurse appeared, beckoning him to follow her. He roused Naomi, and taking her hand, followed, standing for a moment in his daughter's doorway to pray before they approached the bed, horror showing on their faces at the sight of her face. Tears flowed down Naomi's face as she gently touched it, causing Ryanne's head to flip away from her rapidly. Riordan's face grew grim as he stared at her, determination sinking through him that he needed to bring the culprits to justice.

Chapter 30

Shea moved restlessly, his eyes opening and closing, struggling to breathe. He wanted up but a hand on his chest held him in place. He vaguely heard words but couldn't understand them before he slipped back into unconsciousness.

He roused hours lately, clearer in mind, his eyes searching the room. He frowned before he took in that he was free and in a hospital. He tried to rise and sank back, the pain from his side driving darkness in front of his eyes.

He roused once more, hearing his mother's voice.

"Shea? Are you awake now?"

"Mom, go away. I need to sleep." He refused to open his eyes.

"No, Shea. You need to wake up. The doctor's here and needs to see if you can respond."

Shea cracked open his eyes slightly, squinting against the light. "Mom? What time is it?"

"It's six in the morning. And yes, you will stay awake, young man."

"Mom, stop. Please. Just let me speak to the detective. I need to." Shea's vision faded again as he slept, roused once more as his father gently shook him.

"Shea, I have the detective here. He was in the waiting room, hoping to speak with one of you. He's already spoken with Rory."

Shea nodded, swallowing hard against the dryness in his throat. "I know who they are, Dad. I know them. I've done a photo shoot for their company. Look up the Eagle team in my paperwork. It's them. They're the ones."

Samuel shared a look with the detective, who nodded. Shea had just confirmed the direction they had been on in their investigation.

"Dad? Ryanne?" Shea moved restlessly, trying to rise, but unable to, the pain in his side driving him back to a lying position.

"She's alive, son. Alive and here. They won't let anyone see her, other than her parents."

"I need to, Dad. I need to see her. Please?"

"I'll talk to them, but they won't let you move from your bed for a day or so."

"I don't care. Let me up." The detective moved to help Samuel hold Shea down even as the nurse came running with a sedative. It took a few minutes before he settled and slept again.

"Samuel? Can you get me that material?"

His voice grim as he spoke, Samuel nodded. "I can. Wait until Shannon's here and I'll go get it."

"I'll take you. It's too important to risk having fall into the wrong hands." The detective studied Shea. "There's more than just friendship here."

Samuel sighed. "There is. Apparently they became engaged the night before they disappeared. It's Leah I'm concerned about as well."

Shannon looked around as Samuel approached her, beckoning her to follow him.

"Samuel?"

"Shea named the people he thinks are responsible. I need to go find some material he's asked me to find. There will be an officer with him at all times now." He nodded towards where Naomi stood, waiting for Shannon. "I'm told there will be one with Ryanne as well. Let Riordan know what's up."

Shannon nodded. "He's been muttering names in his sleep. I wrote them down." She pulled a paper from her pocket and handed it to the detective. "Here. I pray this helps."

He looked over the list of names, his face becoming more grim as he did so. "This will definitely help." He looked up at the two in front of him. "I will need to talk to him. At some point. When he's more lucid."

Samuel grinned. "That might be a bit. We'll keep you updated." He shared a look with Shannon. "I know you can't say much, but this just seems so odd. Riordan says that other than the pictures they've found, there has been no demand of any kind. No other contact other than the kidnappings. She can't take much more."

The detective shook his head. "No, she can't. I just hope we can solve this soon."

"That's how we're praying." Shannon was looking towards her son's room as she commented, missing the quick look she was given.

Riordan approached as the couple stood, hesitating as to where they should be.

"Samuel? Shannon? Shea? Is he okay?"

Shannon laughed. "He is, I think. He told me he needed to sleep and that's just like him." She studied Riordan. "How is Ryanne?"

Riordan shook his head, unable to speak for a moment. "I want the men responsible. They've hurt her bad. I talked to Rory. He is devastated that he couldn't prevent it from happening." He nodded towards Shea's room. "He will be the same." He turned to lean against the wall. "We aren't any closer, are we?"

"Actually, Shea was muttering some names and he did name a company he thinks is involved." Samuel stared at Shannon. "You know, the detective didn't get that information. Now, I wonder why."

Riordan's face grew stern. "I've had my doubts about him. What material are you meaning?"

Samuel reached to grasp Riordan's arm and pulled him towards the stairs. "Come with me. I want to look at that material. And Shannon had a list of names he was muttering. Can your people do some research?"

"Absolutely. Let me have them and I'll pass the list on to them. They're all angry and fighting mad to put it mildly."

Chapter 31

Two days later, Shea was on his feet and dressed with his father's help.   He simply shook his head at the nurse as she ordered him back to bed, staring her down, simply stating he was going to find his lady love and she was not going to stand in his way. Redmond stood in the shadows, finally shaking his head as he found a wheel chair and approached Shea.

"Sit, Shea. I'll take you to her. I don't think you are up to a walk, even just a few doors down."   Redmond waited as he watched Shea stare between the chair and the door and then at him before he sighed. "Shea? If you don't use this, I won't let you in to see her."

"It's not up to you, Redmond. You can't keep me away from her." Shea moved around the chair and pulled the door open, grimacing with pain as he did so.   He walked towards a door just down the hall from him, his hand running gently along the railing, keeping himself upright by sheer determination.

The nurse stood and watched him, Redmond standing beside her.

"He really did just go and do that? What am I to tell the doctor? He didn't want him moving around too much."

Redmond shrugged even as he grinned. "Unfortunately, what the doctor wants isn't what Shea wants. He needs to be with my sister. She needs him." He walked away, leaving the nurse staring after him before she shook her head and headed for the desk, intent on calling the physician and warning him that Shea was on his feet.

Shea stopped inside the door to Ryanne's room, his eyes sliding closed. He had been so wrong, he thought. Why was I so stubborn, Lord? Redmond only wanted to help and I refused him, like a fool. Now I'm paying the price for that. His eyes opened and he stared at the bed where Ryanne was laying, his eyes lifting to study the medical equipment around her and then dropping to her face, even as he moved closer to her. He heard the door swish open and closed behind him and the sound of

Redmond's feet as he too approached the bed.

Shea stood at the bedside, sorrow shaking him as he watched Ryanne sleep, moving restlessly as she did so. He studied her face, wincing at the dark purple bruising, the swelling, and felt anger rise in him. He tried to tamp it down but couldn't. His mind went back to that last day, when she had been hurt, and how he had tried, Oh, Lord, please, how he had tried to get free and get to her. He hadn't been able to. He knew Rory had tried to. The brutality of the men shocked him even now. He had no idea what they wanted. The words had been too low for him to hear or understand. All he knew was that she had refused to comply with their request.

He reached out a tentative finger, gentle in his touch as he ran it down her face. Redmond watched, amazed, as she turned into Shea's hand where she would flinch away from others. Shea heard her sigh and then her eyelids flickered.

"Redmond?" Her voice was barely audible, pain filling it.

"Right here, hon." He stepped around to the other side of the bed, his hand on her, mindful of the IV line running to it. "Right here."

"Him?" She could barely get her words out. "Shea? Here?"

"He is, hon. That's his hand you're leaning on."

"Kay. Make stay."

"He's not leaving, not anytime soon." Redmond looked up at Shea, finding his friend's eyes steady on Ryanne. "He won't leave you."

"Thought dead."

"No, you're all alive. Rory's around somewhere."

"No. Stay away." She was becoming agitated and the two men shared a glance before Shea reached for her free hand, his own hand warm and strong on hers.

"Rest easy, sweetheart. We won't let them hurt you. Not if we can help it."

"No. Dinosaur." She drifted off to sleep, her face still cradled in Shea's hand.

"Where is she coming up with that? I don't understand." Shea stared down at her, not seeing the look on Redmond's face as he studied his sister's hand. "Redmond?"

"Shea? What did you two go and do?" He lifted her hand, pointing to the ring.

"We got engaged.   Do you have a problem with that?" Shea was ready for a fight but swaying with fatigue and pain.

Redmond gave a sigh and then paced around the bed, finding a chair and shoving Shea into it. "No, I don't have a problem. I'm just not sure this is the right time."

"That's not your decision, is it? We've prayed, a lot, and have peace. We're not rushing into anything." Shea studied the face of the lady he loved. "I need to let her heal. It will take weeks for that."

"Yeah, it will."   Redmond looked around as the door swung open and two men entered. "Well, well. And look who's here. Abe.   Murphy.   What's going on?"   He reached to shake their hands, introducing them to Shea. "These are the men we need to keep you two safe."

Shea just shook his head, his attention back on Ryanne, trying to think through what he knew but too fatigued and sore to do much that way. He faintly heard Redmond and the two men talking before he turned his head, a thought breaking through.

"Redmond, excuse me. That dinosaur in the park. Who funded it? And why? It just seems so odd to have one there. It just doesn't make sense."

Redmond stared at Shea, even as he heard Abe making a call. "You know, Shea. I'm not sure anyone ever said. I'll have Dad or one of the team look into it." He turned as he heard a sound from Murphy. "Murphy? What was that?"

"I said Micah's wife had picked up on that, for some reason. Her mind is scary the way it works. She's tracking that back but it's leading to a succession of numbered companies."

"That is so bizarre. That doesn't make sense." Shea suddenly bent over, the pain driving him from his chair to his knees. The three men were beside him in an instant, hands reaching to raise him and set him into the wheel chair, Redmond heading with it

back to Shea's room. Shea vaguely heard
words but the pain had driven his ability to
think clearly away from him.

Chapter 32

Three days later, Ryanne sat propped up in her hospital bed, the bruising still dark but with green and yellow now mixing in. She squinted at her parents and brothers as they stood around her bed, a frown on her face.

"No. No way." She was adamant she was not going back to her parents, nor to one of her brothers' places, to recover. She just knew if she did, she would bring harm to them and that she wanted to avoid. Rory had already been hurt because of her. And she didn't want anyone else hurt. She cautiously felt the paper she had hidden under her blankets when her family had arrived.

Riordan stared at his daughter. "You need to, Ryanne. You can't be on your own."

She glared at her father, anger working its way through her. "No, Dad. On my own. Not with you." She stared at each one in turn, seeing Regan leaning back against the wall, her eyes compassionate, her face expressionless. Regan knew what she was going through, to some extent, Ryanne knew. "Just leave. All of you, but Regan. Please?" She laid her head back, her eyes closing, fighting against her emotions. She needed to see Shea but he wasn't there. In fact, she had not seen him that day and she was worried about him.

She jumped as a hand came down on hers and then she heard Regan's voice, praying. She relaxed, knowing that Regan was just who she needed with her.

"Can I get you anything, Ryanne?" Regan's voice was low.

"No. I just need to see Shea."

Regan's head turned as she heard the door open and saw Nathaniel, one of Abe's men, entering. "We'll see what we can do about that. I think he's having the chest tube pulled today or some other type of testing. At least, that's what Shannon said."

Ryanne sighed, even as her eyes opened and she saw Nathaniel standing there. She jumped in surprise, not quite sure why he was even in her room. "Nathaniel? Why?"

He simply grinned even as he leaned against the foot of the bed. "Emma asked. That's why." He nodded towards Regan. "She was talking with your sister, who mentioned what had happened. We had some free time and decided to spend it with you and Shea."

She sighed. "No, that's not true." She swallowed against the nausea she had been fighting. "Regan, can you see if you can find me some ginger ale?" Her words weren't as clear as she wanted, given her jaw was wired shut, but Regan nodded, hesitated and then walked from the room.

Nathaniel watched her leave, before his attention went back to Ryanne, his head tilting as he watched her fidgeting.

"When did the letter come?"

Her eyes shot up to him and then she sighed, pulling out a paper from under the blankets. She stared at it. She had read it, crumpled it, uncrumpled it, folded it, unfolded it, went to tear it into pieces, stopped herself from doing that, and then just tucked it away. She handed it to him.

"It was on my pillow this morning, before my family came. Please? Make them stop." She blinked at the tears that she couldn't stop. She jumped once more as she saw the handkerchief appear in her line of sight before she took it, dabbing at her eyes and face.

Nathaniel watched her closely for a moment, knowing just how close she was coming to breaking. "You didn't see anyone or hear anyone?" When she shook her head, he sighed. He would need to talk to Abe. There shouldn't have been anyone but the nurse in her room. That Abe had stressed vehemently.

He unfolded the paper, his eyes still on her, before he looked down, his face settling into grim lines. "You have no idea who?"

"No. I wish I did. I'd make them stop."

He read the letter again. "And you have no idea what they want?"

She shook her head and regretted it, a hand going up to press against her temple.

"No. I don't understand. They haven't made sense. Why beat me up? What is their plan?"

Nathaniel reached for his phone. "I have an idea that I need to run by Abe. Let me talk to him and then I'll talk to you. I promise." He walked away, his voice quiet as he spoke to Abe, before he turned back to her.

"Ryanne, I am going to state something. Don't say anything until you think it through. We have been researching this Mary. We have conclusive evidence that she is dead. A body was found not long after she disappeared. It was kept very quiet but we have had a court order to talk to her parents. That was the only way we could do that. It was her." He watched her closely. "They deny having anything to do with what you've going through. Abe believes them. However, there are family members who do blame you. Her uncle, the one in the photo one of your brothers found in your apartment, was very vocal that you needed to pay for her death." He paused, struggling to know how to express himself.

"They want me dead."

"No, not yet. What it appears they want is for your family to pay, to be destroyed. That is what this is all about. To fracture your closeness. So far, they have been successful. You are withdrawing from your family, thinking to protect them. That doesn't work. It never does."

She stared at the hand she was running across the blanket before her fingers clenched at it. "You're right. We are fractured. How do we heal? What all we've gone through? It's changed us. Changed the dynamics of the family." She looked around him as the door opened and Regan hesitated before she approached. "Regan? Have you seen Shea?"

"I did. He's on his way to see you. They're releasing him today, he said."

"Find my nurse. I'm out of here too. Nathaniel, if you don't mind, find your boss and make some plans. We'll need to find my family as well."

Regan stared at her for a moment before she spun on her heel and almost ran for the nurse, knowing that Ryanne would just leave unless they agreed to discharge her.

Chapter 33

Shea watched Ryanne closely as she sat beside him, his arm around her. They were both hurting, he knew, but there was something different about her that afternoon. She had asked him to meet her at her parents, and yes, she wanted his parents there as well. Time had come, she informed him, to take back their lives.

His attention turned to the other men in the room, standing back, but watchful. Regan had mentioned that some friends had stopped in to help but he wasn't sure that they were necessary, even though the Stuart family seemed to think they were.

Abe stood back, watching, ready to speak his mind when he had a chance before he shared a glance with Murphy, who simply shook his head. There was more going on here than they knew about.

Abe finally walked towards where Riordan and Samuel stood, deep in conversation, a hand going up to touch Riordan's shoulder.

Riordan turned, a frown on his face, knowing Abe would not interrupt him unless he felt it necessary.

"Abe?"

"Can you have your family stop bickering for a moment and then let us talk? This isn't getting you anywhere. In fact, I would suggest we spend the next while in prayer."

Riordan stared at him, then nodded, before he turned to his family, seeing what Abe was seeing. Samuel stood, his eyes on his son, hurting for him.

"All right, my family. Let's be quiet for a moment." Riordan's commanding voice broke through the various conversations and stopped them all, causing his family to stare at him. "We need to stop this bickering and fighting among ourselves. This is what they've wanted, I suspect. Find a partner. It's prayer time."

They watched him for a moment before exchanging glances and doing what he had asked. This was something they had been lax in doing, and they knew that.

An hour later, refreshed in mind and spirit, Riordan stood once more in front of the fireplace, his gaze shifting from one to another, before resting the longest on Ryanne and Shea. His eyes raised to meet Naomi, who nodded.

"Okay, folks. Abe has something to say, I suspect. Abe?"

Abe nodded, his eyes too searching each face before he looked back at Riordan and then Samuel. "I do. Emma's been busy and has sent a raft of material for us to look through. You are correct, Riordan, when you stated that they were trying to break up your family. And from my point of view, they've been doing that. Ryanne, I know you want to stand on your own two feet. It's a given. But work with us, please? Work with your family. Don't go off on your own. That's what they're waiting for. This last time? It could very easily have killed you. If that is part of the plan, then the next time likely will. Do you understand?"

She nodded, knowing it was true, her hand tightening on Shea's. She couldn't comment, she was only too well aware of how she felt.

"Now, we need to come up with a plan." Abe turned to Samuel and Shannon. "I know you, Samuel. We've worked together in the past. What are your thoughts?"

"We can't wrap the two in bubblewrap and stick them away. That won't solve anything." Samuel heard Shea's groan at that. "Seriously, Shea, we need to come up with a plan and soon. This is escalating, and I suspect will culminate in the next week to ten days."

Abe was nodding as was Riordan. "That's our feeling. Now, about this dinosaur?" He turned to Ryanne. "Do you have any idea what that's all about?"

She started to shake her head, then stopped, a thoughtful look on her face, before her eyes slid closed and she groaned. "Mary. She was obsessed with dinosaurs. She wanted to become a palaeontologist, but her parents were opposed to that. She used to do things on the sly, without telling them what she was up to. She had a whole series of books and material on them. What happened to that?"

"We asked her parents. They knew about it but never said anything to her. It disappeared after she died. They have no idea who took it."

"Try her uncle." Ryanne rested her head on Shea's shoulder, exhausted from the effort of speaking.

"We would, if we could find him. He disappeared a number of weeks ago."

Shea looked down at Ryanne and then at Riordan. "About the time all this started? And is he the one responsible for the dinosaur statue in the park?"

Riordan's hand froze as he lifted his mug of coffee to drink from before he set it carefully down on the mantle and then ran his hands down his face. "We are still working through that but I would hazard a guess you're correct on that."

Abe waved his phone, just receiving a text from Jace, Emma's employee. "Jace has finally broken through the barriers set up around that. It was her uncle. Now, where is he?"

"Look around in the woods, I think." Redmond finally spoke. "I vaguely remember hearing that he had a cabin hidden somewhere out there. I've tried tracing it but can't find it."

Nathaniel spoke up. "I think Emma's was working on that. Or Micah was." He shared a look with Micah, who nodded.

"We're tracing that, Redmond. But as you said, it's not easy. This man either has a lot of money or a lot of friends." Micah's quiet voice broke into Rory's thoughts.

"I think neither." Rory looked up. "I remember him. He was a loner, was never seen with anyone. Unless he's changed I doubt that he's had a lot of help."

"I think he has, Rory." Regan finally spoke. "I know he gave that impression, but I used to see him with a group of men. They were ones that always seemed to be into crime."

Ryanne rose, paced from the room, Shea watching before he was on his feet, following her. He found her standing in the kitchen, staring out the back door, her arms wrapped around herself. She turned as he approached, walking into his hug.

"Where do we go from here, Shea?"

"I don't know, sweetheart, but your family? Abe? They'll come up with a plan."

"That is sure to involve sticking me away somewhere. I won't do that." She winced as the pain in her face and jaw intensified.

Shea reached for her pain medication she had placed on the counter and handed her a glass of water. She frowned and then downed the medications in short order. She knew it would make her sleepy, it always did, and she hated that.

Shea turned her away from the room the others were in and found her father's office, tucking her under a blanket on the couch and then sliding to the floor to sit beside her, a hand cradling his ribs. They were healing, the lung had returned to normal size, but he was hurting for his lady.

Chapter 34

Shea finally rose, his eyes on Ryanne as she slept, then walked away, hoping to find Redmond. He needed to talk to his friend, and on his own. He had a thought he needed to run by him and he didn't want anyone else to hear at that point.

Redmond looked up from the papers he was studying. He thought everyone else had left, but he knew Abe had left two of his men somewhere around the place, as were some of his father's men. They were taking no chances with Ryanne and Shea, that was a given.

"Shea? How are you feeling?"

Shea sighed as he slid down into a chair. "I'm hurting, Redmond, more than I want anyone to know. They did a number on me."

"I know they did. They were using you to get to Ryanne." He sat back, his eyes on the papers in front of him. "I just don't get it."

"I don't think we're supposed to. That's part of their plan. Keep us confused so when the big hit comes, we're not expecting it."

"Abe said something along that lines after you two walked away. Dad and your Dad are trying to come up with a plan, but they're at a loss. Did you know that Ryanne received a threat in the hospital?"

Shea shook his head. "It doesn't surprise me that she wouldn't tell us. Who found out?"

"Nathaniel. He read her correctly. The letter was vague to a point, but it threatened all of us in some way. Dad's working on that. So's your Mom." He paused, not quite sure how to proceed.

"What are your thoughts, Redmond? The detective?"

"That's right. He doesn't seem to have worked very hard on this."

"No, he hasn't. I did some research on him. He's not who he seems. In fact, I would say he's a plant. He's only been on the force for about a year. No one can figure out how he got the vacant detective position. There were others more qualified than he was. This has caused a lot of resentment in the force."

"You never said anything."

"No, I didn't. I couldn't before, but I have a friend who did some research. I left it on your Dad's desk, but the gist of it is? He's not qualified to be a police officer. Never has been. His resume was dummied up."

"And just how did he get on the force?" Redmond could feel the anger rising, knowing it was fruitless, but still he was angry.

"Mom's talking to the police chief today. She's asking for another detective to take over. The thing of it is, he seems to have disappeared." He pulled out his phone as he felt it vibrate. "Mom just sent a text message." His face paled even more than it was as he read it.

"Shea? What does she say? Shea?"

Shea finally looked at Redmond. "He's dead."

"Who's dead?   Shea, you're not making sense."

"The detective. They found his body in his car outside of town.   Wait, she's sending more." He groaned. "He's Mary's cousin."

"It's no wonder, then, we felt like we were getting nowhere.   We were being played, weren't we?"   Redmond rose, hunting for his own phone. "I need to call Dad."

Shea shook his head.   "He knows. He's with Mom and Dad."

"That's where he disappeared to then. I wondered. Now what?" Redmond looked down at the papers he had been working through, then shoved away from the table to pace.

"We can't keep this from her.   You know that."   Shea turned his head as he heard footsteps.   "Ryanne?   You were asleep."

"I know.   What can't you keep from me?"

"The detective."   Shea hesitated for a moment.

"I know. He's related to Mary. I finally figured out who he looks like. When do we talk to him again?"

Shea reached for her hand and drew her down to a chair beside him. "We can't, sweetheart. He's dead."

She stared between Shea and Redmond for a few moments. "Well, I guess that's that then. Find her uncle and you'll solve this."

"Not so quick." They looked around as Rory and Regan approached them.

"What do you mean, not so quick?"

"It gets worse, people. Much worse."

Ryanne paled even more than she had been. "Her brother? The one who ran away before she died?"

Rory gave a grim nod. "He's been involved. He's kept in the shadows, but he's in town. His parents haven't seen him. I talked to them. He hasn't been in touch for years. They can't figure out why."

They all stared at Ryanne as she snorted, then gave a groan of pain. "Now, why'd I go and do that?" She stared at

Shea. "He was into crime and drugs and who knows what all. He was very careful not to let his parents know, but Mary did. I think that's why she was killed. He did it to her. I thought I saw him there that day."

"And you never ever said anything?" Redmond sat beside her, his hand on her arm.

"No, because I wasn't sure. Even now, I'm not, but it's what he would do. He would torment us at times."

Redmond shared a look with his siblings. "Regan, did you know?"

She shook her head. "I don't think anyone of us did."

Chapter 35

Ryanne paced the living room once more. She sighed. This was becoming a habit, wasn't it, Lord? When will this be all over? I want to move on with my life and can't. She paused as she stared at the book shelves, before she moved towards them, reaching for a picture. As loud a scream as she could manage escaped her as the picture fell from her hands to the dark hardwood floor, the glass shattering.

Redmond hit the room on a run, Regan behind him. He stared at Ryanne, before he searched the room, coming to stand in front of her, reaching to hug her.

"Ryanne? What happened."

Trembling, she pointed at the floor. "There. That picture. How did it get here? It's Mary brother, Marcus."

"Her brother?" Redmond stopped to study the picture, before Regan handed him a bag. "Thanks, Regan." He stood, the picture safe in the bag, and stared around. "How did it get in here?"

"Someone keeps tampering with our security system. None of us are safe." Regan moved rapidly away, searching the house, and not finding an entry point. She returned, to find Redmond on his knees, hands feeling along the book shelf before they heard a click and the shelf moved towards them.

"Redmond? What did you do?" Regan stared at the opening that appeared.

"I just wondered if there was something. Given that Leah had secret passages all over her house."

"But she was near the lake and there was smuggling. When did this happened? I remember when the shelves were built. There was nothing like this then." Regan moved closer, peering into the dimness.

"No, there wasn't. We need to find Dad and find him now." Redmond had his phone out, dialling his father's number. "Dad? I found the entry point. I need you here now. I'm at your place."

Riordan stood, staring just as his family had done, trying to think through the consequences of what they had found. Abe stood inside the cavity, a large flashlight in his hand illuminating the area.

"Abe?"

"Let my men search it through. That way you all stay safe." Abe nodded at four of his men as they moved past him, grim looks on their faces. "You had absolutely no idea?"

"None. I don't think any of us did." Riordan looked around as he heard Rory's voice. "Now why is Rory here?"

Rory and Leah hesitated as they entered, their eyes on the book shelf.

"You've found it already, have you?" Leah moved towards it, Riordan's hand stopping her from going forward. "I came across some notes of Dad's. He knew this house, apparently. I never knew that. He mentioned a secret passage. This must be it."

Riordan stared at her. "You're just telling us now?"

"Ease up, Dad. She just found the diary again this morning. She had no reason to connect the house with us until now." Rory's eyes were on Ryanne, watching as she paced, a hand to her face.

"R o r y ?   F i n d   S h e a please?" Ryanne's quiet voice was barely heard before she ran from the room.

Redmond stared after her and then reached for his phone. "Shea will never believe this. I just know that."

Shea found Ryanne an hour later, sliding down on the couch beside her, and wrapping her in his arms. His chin rested on the top of her head as he waited for her to speak.

"Why, Shea? What does he want?"

"Revenge?"

She sighed. "No, that's not his style. He's cold and calculating.   There's something more than that involved."

"I haven't seen the photo. What was it?"

"You and me. Near the dinosaur. Are we never to be free of that?"

"Soon, sweetheart. Soon." He grew silent, puzzling over what had happened. "Is there anything else you can remember?"

She nodded. "The dinosaur? It was him. He always bragged that this town was oldfashioned and a dinosaur. He was going where there was more action. But I don't get it. Why?"

"We'll ask him that when we see him. On another note, Mom has spoken with the police chief and pulled some strings. We have a new detective on our case and he wants to speak with us."

"Who?"

"Edgar Grenville." He tightened his hold as she shoved at him. "Ryanne? What's wrong?"

"Not him. He's a friend of Marcus'. I know him from when we were young. I can't speak with him. I won't."

"Well, then, you won't."

Reilly appeared in the room at that point, looking behind him before he spoke. "Ryanne? What was that you said?"

She repeated her words, and Reilly shook his head.

"I thought he looked familiar. Come on. You two are out of here. I'll explain to Mom and Dad later."

Ryanne was on her feet, following her brother, Shea right behind her. The door closed softly after them, even as Naomi came looking for them, puzzlement on her face when she didn't find them. She turned to apologize to the detective, to be met with a gun pointed at her.

"Sit, Mrs. Stuart. You'll not be going looking for them."

"What is going on? You're with the police. You can't do this."

"I can and I will. Harbouring fugitives I think is the charge."

Chapter 36

Ryanne watched through the partly closed door as the house was searched and her family dragged from various rooms and shoved into chairs. She froze, feeling Shea's arm around her and knowing Reilly was beside her.

"Reilly? What now? They have Mom, Rory and Leah, and Aideen. We have to get them out of there."

"And we will." Reilly shot a glance around and then pulled Ryanne with him, heading for the door to the garage. "Through here. We should be able to get outside, I think."

He hesitated for a moment, and then shoved Ryanne and Shea through the outside door. "Run for the shed, Ryanne. Take cover there. I'll be behind you as soon as I can. Reach Dad and let him know." The door closed quietly behind him as the two ran for the shed.

"Shea? What now?"

"Now, we call your Dad and mine. We need to keep them from appearing. Then, we try and find some way to help."

"I know, but neither of us is up to doing much." She sank back against the shed wall, her eyes on the window in the door. "Won't they search here?"

"I suspect they already have. We need to let Reilly work his magic. Isn't that what he does best?"

"It is. I just don't like it."

"No one said you had to." A finger on her lips stilled any further conversation and he quickly drew her back behind piles of furniture already stored for the winter.

They heard the rough conversation of the two men who appeared and stood in the doorway, not entering any further. Ryanne's hand gripped Shea's tighter and he looked down at her, seeing the knowledge in her face that she knew the men.

"I know them. They're Marcus' friends as well. Will we never be free of them?"

Shea slid to the ground, pulling her down with him, his phone out as it vibrated. He listened and knew the men had walked away but he wasn't sure how far they had gone.

"It's your Dad. He's on the road out front. Dad's with him. They're working to find a way to get in and rescue your family."

"Tell him Marcus is likely here." She slumped back against the wall. "We have to do something, Shea."

"I know, but we can't be seen." He lifted his eyes.   "We need to pray, sweetheart, pray like we never have before. God is here. He will protect them and us." He listened as he heard faint footsteps and grew quiet, not moving and keeping Ryanne from moving as well.

A form appeared in front of them, causing them both to jump, until they realized it was Reilly.

"Reilly?   You scared me." Ryanne's tone was disgruntled.

He grinned. "Sorry. I wasn't sure you were still here."   He dropped to a sitting position beside them. "They've taken them away. I saw the van leaving."

"All of them?"

Reilly shook his head. "No. I think Mom and Regan. I didn't see Rory or Leah go with them."

"Then, get into the house and find them." Ryanne surged to her feet, not waiting for the men, and was through the door and back into the garage, her hand on the house door when Shea's hand on it stopped her from opening it. She glared up at him.

"Wait, Ryanne. Wait for our Dads. We need them."

She slumped against the door, defeat coursing through her. "We need to go in, Reilly. We can't wait."

"We have to, Ryanne. You're not fit. Nor is Shea." Reilly's head turned as he heard movement behind the door. "Away from there and behind the truck." He shoved her roughly down, Shea crouching beside her.

Shea listened and then rose. "Rory? Leah?"

Rory spun, his fists up until he recognized Shea. "You two are okay?"

"We are. And you?"

"We're fine, but I need to get Leah to the hospital."

Ryanne stared at him for a moment and then turned her eyes to Leah. "Leah?"

"Just some cramping, Ryanne. Nothing to worry about, but overly-concerned Daddy-to-be wants it checked out."

They turned as the garage doors opened and men poured in, police officers among them. Rory and Leah were whisked away separately from the other three.

Riordan watched his son and daughter and then sighed. Lord, why? Wasn't it enough that three had to go through this? Now Ryanne. I would have wanted her to avoid this.

"Dad?" Reilly spoke from beside him. "Any word on Mom and Regan?"

Riordan nodded.   "The van was stopped. They're in negotiations right now, but it's not Marcus who took them."

"It wasn't? Then who?"

"Mary's father. He wants revenge on us. I thought he had been okay."

"So, did I. This is really going to hurt Ryanne."

"Tell me about it.   How are those two?"

"They're hurting, Dad. Ryanne needs to be in bed. She's refusing to go, and Shea won't relax until she does."

"Let's see if we can at least get her laying down in one of the rooms." Riordan was worried, trying not to show it, but knowing things could go drastically wrong for his wife and daughter.

Chapter 37

Naomi ran for Riordan as she saw him waiting near the police tape surrounding the van. She could hear Regan's sobs as she was enveloped in Delaney's arms.

"Ryanne? The others?"

"They're safe, my dear." Riordan swept her away, his eyes on the officers surrounding them. "Let's get you home."

"They're okay? I was so worried. I know Reilly and Ryanne and Shea had disappeared. They tried to tell us they had them."

"Not at all." Riordan slid into the backside of the SUV, watching as Regan and Delaney did the same to another one. "Reilly got them out, hid them in the shed out back, and then found them."

"What aren't you telling me?"

Riordan gave a big sigh. He should have know that he couldn't hide anything from her. "They're fine, my dear. Reilly said it was Marcus' father who did this."

"I know, but what about our family?"

"Okay. Rory took Leah to the hospital to be assessed. He called a few minutes ago. They're heading home. Leah has to rest and he says she can't with all the excitement at our place."

"Excitement? Is that what he calls it?" Naomi was out of the vehicle almost before it stopped, running for the open door and then her family, clutching each one to her, before she hugged Ryanne even tighter, her arm going out to gather Shea to them.

"Thank you, Shea. Now, let's get you two sitting down somewhere. You'll never heal like this."

"Mother!" Ryanne's voice was faint and she knew her face was pounding, but she had to find out what happened. "What happened?"

"Sit, sweetheart. Your brother bringing in sandwiches and coffee for us. Your mom needs a moment to recover."

She nodded, finally sinking down on the couch, her feet tucked up under her, Shea's arm around her. "I just want to know. I want to know why."

"He's not talking, Ryanne. He has refused to. But I overheard him say someone asked him to do this. It's was directed at your father, not you." Naomi turned a puzzled glance towards Riordan. "And I don't know why."

Riordan looked up as Reilly approached, a sheaf of papers in his hand. "Reilly? What have you there?"

"Information we should have had before, Dad. Maybe some of this might not have happened." He looked with sorrow at his sister and Shea. "I'm sorry, you two. We should have known what's in this. You wouldn't have been hurt if we had."

Ryanne stared at him and then turned her eyes to her father, watching as his face grew stern, and knowing something was up.

"Dad?"

"How many times are we going to have to go back to that last trip Rory and Regan went on? Is it going to haunt us forever?" Riordan was on his feet, moving quickly from the room, the papers waving in his hand.

"Reilly? What did you give Dad?" Regan spoke from where she had curled up next to Ryanne.

"Information about that last trip. It was a set up. I just got confirmation of that. It's taken all this time to track down the people in the other country, get them to talk, get them to give statements, and then confirm the evidence. We still don't know who's behind it, but we're getting closer."

"That trip?" Regan shared a look with Ryanne. "I thought it was over and done with."

"Apparently not." Reilly slumped in his chair, his eyes on his mother, who sat, head bowed, fatigue evident. "Mom, you need to go lay down."

Naomi looked up, a smile on her face. "I will, Reilly. Soon. It's just I don't want to leave any of you, not just yet."

Chapter 38

Two weeks later, Shea sat at his desk, concentrating on his photos. He had been out again, doing photo shoots, Ryanne with him as much as she could be, not wanting to be with her family, but still working for her father. She had refused to take time off to heal, much to his dismay.

Shea stared at his monitor, before he shoved away from his desk, and rose, to pace through his house. His parents had moved to their own place weeks before, and he was alone. He stared at the rooms, seeing the dated furniture, old paint and wallpaper, and worn-out drapes. He turned in a circle before he was almost running for the door. That was what he would do, he thought. To keep Ryanne near him, he would have her plan an update to the rooms. He could afford whatever she chose, knowing she would be frugal, almost too much so.

Ryanne stared at him for a moment before she hugged him, rising from behind her desk, and walking away, not seeing her father staring after her before he sighed and headed for her office. She needed to do this, he thought. She needs to decide where she wants to be.

He turned instead, heading to find Redmond. They had never finished that conversation they had started weeks ago, and they needed to.

Ryanne finally stared at her father late that afternoon, as he stood in Shea's office, his hands on her shoulders.

"Dad? What are you saying? Are you firing me?" She was perplexed, not quite sure of what he meant. All she knew was that her life had been upturned too much lately.

"Not at all. I want you to follow your dreams. They have never been truly with the company. Redmond and I have been talking. We're planning on taking the firm a different way. He was quite impressed with Abe's company."

Ryanne's face lit up and she tried hard to yell, but could only get out a squeak. "Training, Dad? You're talking training?

Wonderful! And Shea can help." She spun, running towards his arms, and hugging him. "You will, won't you?"

"Help how?" He grinned at Riordan, having a good suspicion of where she was heading.

"Now, hold on, Ryanne. It's still up in the air. We have commitments over the next few weeks that we need to look at. Then we have a lot of planning to do."

She smirked at her father from the safety of Shea's arms. "Look in my top desk drawer. You'll find a folder. I already have been."

Riordan stared at her and then joined Shea in laughter. "Ahead of me, are you? Can't say as I blame you. How much longer until the wires come out?"

"Two weeks. I can't wait." She sobered. "Dad, will we find them soon?"

"We're doing our best, honey. The new detective is a wonder. She's dug up a lot of material, and that Emma has been shooting her everything she can find."

"Emma's good. I want this over, Dad. I want to go on with my life. Mom and I are making plans, but we can't even set a date, not while this is hanging over our heads." She leaned back against Shea.

"Don't let that deter you. If you want to go ahead when you're free of the jaw wires, talk to me. We'll make it happen." He watched them for a moment before he walked away, knowing that Ryanne and Shea were near to setting a date. He prayed for their safety over the next weeks, knowing it had come to a crisis for them.

Shea walked out with Riordan, hesitating for a moment. "Where do we stand, do you know, with the investigation?"

Riordan shrugged. "I wish I had better news. They are still searching for the uncle and the son. Her father hasn't said much. In fact, he has refused to speak even to his lawyer. That's not sitting well with anyone."

"He's scared, Riordan. Scared and trying not to give way."

"I suspect you're right. Listen, what Ryanne asked? If you are interested in coming aboard, let me know. We don't want to take you away from what you are doing now."

Shea just grinned. "She makes a good case, but I enjoy what I'm doing." He watched as Riordan drove away, turning as he sensed Ryanne beside him. "Got all your plans made, sweetheart?"

She shrugged. "I'm not sure, Shea. Not sure where to start first."

"Where your heart says to." He hugged her to him, his chin resting on her head. "How be we set it aside for now?"

"I'd like that. I want to work on our mystery instead."

"You do, do you? And just what do you think you'll find that the others won't."

"Because I know Mary and I knew Marcus. I have insight into them the others don't. Not even Regan knows what I know."

"Then, I guess I sit you down at the computer and let you type away, putting down your thoughts and impressions."

She paused in her walk. "No one has ever suggested that. Why not?"

Chapter 39

Three weeks later, Ryanne was free from the wires in her jaw, the bruising and swelling on her face was mostly gone, and her eye had been declared just fine. She looked up from her desk in the family office building as Redmond shut the door behind him and then perched on the corner of her desk, his eyes on his hands.

When he didn't speak, she finally asked him what was up.

He shrugged. "Dad let me have the paperwork you gave him a couple of weeks ago. You were very thorough, Ryanne. Why didn't we know all this before?"

She shrugged. "I didn't see the point. Mary was dead. Marcus was gone. Who would have thought this would have come back to trouble us." She searched her desk. "I found this the other night when I was sorting through old high school stuff." She handed him a notebook. "It was one of Marcus'. I don't know what's in it. I have no way of knowing how I got it."

Redmond's hand froze as he reached for it and he groaned even as his eyes slid shut. "Ryanne? Did it occur to you this is what they're after?"

"That? No. Should it have?"

"Well, yeah. They wanted some kind of treasure from you, didn't they?"

"They asked for a box or a chest. That's not either one."

Redmond held up the book, showing her the front cover. "And what is on the front of it?"

She squinted. "A box. So what?"

"Ryanne!"

She stared at her brother and then back at the book. "A box? This is the treasure box they wanted? That's not a box, it's a book."

"Which happens to have a box on the front. Of course, it's what they're after." Redmond was on his feet, his hand drawing his sister to her feet as well, and then tugging her with him towards their father's office.

Riordan looked up as Redmond and Ryanne flew into his office, sitting back and dropping his pen to the desktop.

"What is going on? You two came in here like you were running from a fire."

"Not quite, Dad. Ryanne just gave me this. This is what they're after. This book."

Riordan carefully reached for it, his eyes on his daughter. "You didn't know you had it, did you?"

"No, I didn't, Dad. If I hadn't been sorting out paperwork and stuff from school, I not likely would have found it."

Riordan nodded, knowing she would have turned it over to them earlier if she had found it. "And what's so special about it?"

She shrugged. "I have no idea. All I know is that Mary had it one day and then I found it the other day. I didn't know she had left it with me." She stopped. "Is that why she was killed?"

Riordan was glancing through the book, his face growing sterner with each page he turned. "I suspect so. Does anyone know you have it?"

"Other than you and Redmond? No."

"And don't tell anyone. I'm taking a copy of it and then the police detective will be given it." He looked up at Ryanne. "This means you are still in grave danger."

"I know that, Dad. Until we find them, I will be."

Redmond followed her with his eyes as she walked away. "Dad, what didn't you say?"

"I don't think she understands just how deep in crime he was when he was a teenager. He was setting himself up to take over a druglord's territory. If he tried that and succeeded, then he's put all of us in danger. He names Ryanne in here as well as his sister."

Redmond sank back in his chair. "Then, how do we go about this? How do we keep her safe? We can't stick her away somewhere. She'll run first."

"I know. And somehow this has to be related to that last trip. I see similar names in the book."

"Will we never be free of that?"

"I pray we are. Redmond, go. Find your sister and stay with her, at least for the rest of the day. I want her back at the house tonight, and I know she'll fight me on that. She already informed me that Shea and she had plans for tonight."

"They do. I think it was to meet with the minister or something like that."

"The minister? Lovely." Riordan sat back and then reached for his phone. "Let me talk to Shea and see what he says. If we have to, the minister can come to our place."

Redmond stood for a moment, his eyes on his sister, until she looked up and sighed.

"Come on in, Redmond. It looks as if I have a babysitter."

He shook his head. "No, just a concerned brother."

She glared at him and then sighed. "Redmond, why?"

He shrugged. "We'll ask them when we catch them."

"And you're sure we'll do that?"

"I am. Dad wants you at the house tonight." He held up his hand as she protested. "He's calling Shea. They'll work it out."

"I hate this, you know." She sighed again. "God needs to work on my attitude, doesn't He? And don't bother answering.

Chapter 40

Shea stood in front of the dinosaur statue, a puzzled look on his face. Something was different about it, and he wasn't sure what. He felt Ryanne tug at his arm.

"Shea, staring at it won't change a thing."

"There's something different about it, Ryanne. What is it?"

She moved around it. "I don't see anything different. Wait! What this?" She reached out a hand, Shea's hand stopping hers. "Shea?"

"That crack wasn't there before. What caused it?" He suddenly grabbed her hand tight and pulled her with him, back into the trees surrounding it as he heard footsteps heading their way.

He listened to the men's conversation, then caught the look on Ryanne's face and sighed. Marcus must be out there. He peeked through the leaves, watching as the crack she had found widened as the leg of the dinosaur moved and then the men disappeared through the opening, the leg moving back to hide the spot.

Ryanne stared at it, then at him. "Did we really see what we saw?"

"We did. Come on. Let's get out of here."

They moved quickly away, heading for his truck, stopping as they saw men surrounding it.

"They've found your truck, Shea. Now what?"

He looked around, and then pulled her hurriedly after him, running for the other end of the park. He finally stopped, breathing hard, and looking around.

"Here. Sit on this bench. I'm calling in reinforcements."

Redmond and Reilly appeared shortly, walking up to them, questions on their faces.

"The dinosaur, Redmond. It opens. We saw it. Marcus was there."

Redmond stared at her, then whisked her away to his car, tucking her into the backseat. Shea stood outside for a moment, his eyes on the parking lot he could see from there.

"They were around my truck, Redmond. Who they were, I have no idea?"

"We saw them. They scattered when some vehicles pulled in." Redmond ducked his head to watch his sister, even as he heard Reilly on the phone, speaking with the authorities. "We need to get you two out of here. They don't need to know you saw them."

"My truck?"

"I'll find some excuse to have it towed to a friend's garage. Didn't you say yesterday you wanted to get the brakes checked?"

Shea stared at him before he grinned and shook his head. "I did, but not at this very moment."

"It happens now, Shea. Now, into the car. We're leaving. I'll meet my friend somewhere and turn your keys over to him."

Shea nodded, his keys quickly dropped into Redmond's open hand. "Home, then, James."

Redmond glared at him. "Just to set the record straight, I am not your chauffeur."

"You're not? You could have fooled me.

Later that evening, Ryanne watched as the detective settled himself into a chair, accepting with a grin of thanks the mug of coffee and sandwich handed to him.

"Thank you. I haven't had time to eat since this morning."

"Go ahead and eat then." Naomi perched on a chair, anxious to hear what he had to say. "You need to keep your strength up."

"Thank you. Not many people take into account that we're human."

The detective, Ross Adams, as he introduced himself, finally set aside his mug, his eyes on Ryanne.

"Ryanne? How are you?"

She shrugged. "Ready to have this over with, thank you very much. I have plans I want to get to."

Ross laughed. "I hear tell you do. Now, let's see. Where did we leave it when we last spoke?"

"I have no idea. Dad said he had given you the notebook."

"Yes, that notebook. It was all you thought and more. We'll preparing charges against him based on our investigations from that." He looked around the room. "To put your minds at ease, we arrested Marcus and four of his friends today. You're being there, Ryanne and Shea? That solved a mystery for us. We had been told by an informant that they were hiding in town. No one thought that it was in that statue. They had quite the set up. Beds, a kitchen, even a shower of sorts. They could stay there and not be seen. In fact, it was tunneled down beneath the surface.”

“It was? I’d like to see that.” Ryanne sat forward. “But does this end it for us?”

Ross shook his head. “Unfortunately, not. We still have to find the uncle. Marcus’ father was informed with his lawyer present that his son was arrested. He began to talk. He was living in fear of him. He knew Marcus had killed his sister and had threatened both his parents. His mother was not aware of that. We’ll be bringing her in to talk with as well.”

“How? How could he do that? And why?” Ryanne leaned into Shea, sudden fear coursing through her. “Is he the one?”

“The one?”

She nodded, her eyes on the detective. “I have been followed for years. I would find flat tires, broken windows, whatever on my vehicle. I thought it was vandals. It had to be him. Threatening me.”

"It was. We found evidence in his paperwork, which we are still working through and will be for quite a while."

"Why?"

"From what we can determine, he thought you saw him that day. That you were searching for him when you were searching for Mary. It was because of him that her parents never went public with her death. Her father insisted on that. He was afraid for them but he was also afraid for you, for Regan, and then the rest of your family. Marcus had been very specific with his threats."

"But you can't guarantee that he won't direct anything from jail?" Riordan spoke finally, his eyes on his daughter.

"No, we can't guarantee that." Ross paused as his voice vibrated and he looked down at it. "If you will excuse, I need to take this call." He walked away, leaving a stunned silence behind him.

"Dad, did you know?" Regan's voice was barely audible as Delaney wrapped an arm around her.

"I had a suspicion after seeing the notebook. What you all didn't know was that Marcus accounted for every move he made, every robbery, every threat, every drug deal, and yes, every murder. And there was more than one murder. He has a cold black heart."

They all looked up as the detective returned, distress he was trying to cover by rubbing at his forehead,

"Ross?" Redmond spoke for the group. "You have news?"

"Not the news you want to hear. Marcus was murdered tonight in his cell. We have an inmate in custody. And his father is in the hospital, also assaulted, and not expected to survive."

"The uncle?" Ryanne's voice held conviction.

"That's what we suspect. I'm sorry, Ryanne. We'll not likely ever know for sure why he targeted you like he did. From what we have found in our investigation, he was behind your kidnappings, except the first one. That one was bizarre. No one associated with him seems to have been involved in it."

"Then who?" Ryanne stared around at her family. "His uncle? Or someone from that last trip?"

Ross shook his head. "You've told me about that trip. I think you may be on to something, but we have no idea who it might be. Again, I'm sorry."

Chapter 41

Ryanne stared at the man standing in front of her, anger sparking from her, yet fear lurked underneath.

"No, I will not go with you." She backed away, her hand reaching for the door knob, twisting it and then slamming the door shut behind her and shooting home the bolts and locks. She sank to the floor, back braced to the door. The uncle had found her. She buried her head on her knees, her arms wrapped around them, her thoughts chaotic.

She didn't hear the sounds of his pounding at the door, his calls for her to open it up, that he needed to talk with her. She didn't hear the sounds of the sirens, or the calls for the man to step away from the door and drop to his knees. She didn't hear his protests that he didn't mean to harm her. He just needed to talk to her. He was innocent. He had been set up.

Redmond found his sister, dropping down beside her, an arm wrapped around her.

"We have the uncle, Ryanne.   It's over."

She looked up at that point, her eyes fixed in the distance.   "No, it's not over. That's not him.   That's not the voice I heard."   She turned to her brother, seeing Shea crouched in front of her. "He's not the one from that building, that first time. There was a woman there."   She paled as she remembered and then her eyes rolled back as her consciousness fled.

Shea reached to scoop her up, heading for the office, laying her down gently, even as Redmond called for Regan.

Regan sat back on her heels after assessing her sister, not able to rouse her. She looked up at the two men hovering over them.

"What happened?"   When neither answered, she was on her feet. "Redmond? Shea? What happened?"

Redmond shrugged.   "The uncle showed up. I found her on the floor against the door.   When I said it was over, she denied it." He looked at Shea. "At least, I think that's what she did."

"She did. She said he wasn't the one in the initial kidnapping and that there had been a woman there." He knelt beside the couch, his hand resting on Ryanne's, feeling hers turn to grasp his. "Ryanne? Can you hear me? Can you wake up?"

"I can hear you. I"m awake."

"You are?   You certainly don't look like you are."

She shoved to a sitting position, her hand still in his. "I am. Regan? Do you remember the other uncle?   The one who was a half-brother to Mary's mother?"

"I do. I never liked him." She sank to the coffee table, her face paling. "It's him? Then that means her mother is involved?"

"That's what I think.   How do we prove it? We can't go to the detective with just a gut feeling."

"No, we can't." Regan looked up at Redmond, watching him closely. "Redmond? How do we prove it?"

"Let me have his name and I'll talk to Emma. She's been working on something for me. This might just be it."

He was off and then back in a few moments, papers in his hands. "She was ahead of us. This is what she's found." He handed them copies.

Shea sat, his arm around his lady, watching intently as she flipped through the papers.

"Emma's good, Regan. But there is still something missing."

"I know. I wish I could remember what." Regan paced, her arms wrapped around herself before she spun, to come and sit beside Ryanne, her hand reaching for her sister's. "Ryanne, wasn't there another uncle or aunt or something?"

Ryanne shook her head. "No, just the one. Her father was an only child. Her mother only had a brother and then a half-brother. No, wait. That's not right. He was a step-brother." Her head went back as she groaned. "I can't remember, Regan, and it's so important that I do."

"I know." Regan rose, walking from the room, returning with a folder. "I was doing research on them. I didn't get as far as Emma, but I think I found some other people."

Redmond reached for the folder, glancing through it. "You're good too, Regan. Between you and Emma, it looks as if you've determined who all is involved." He handed the folder to Shea who looked first at Regan and then Ryanne.

"Ryanne?"

She jerked as she heard his voice, having not really been listening to the conversation going on around her, looking up at him. "Redmond? Where's your last year high school yearbook? Did you take it to your place or leave it here?"

Redmond stared at her, not sure what she was up to.

"Redmond? Where is it?" When he didn't move, she was on her feet, heading for his old room. They could hear her running footsteps as she made her way to the second floor and then almost stumbling as she came back down. Shea was on his feet, his hand outstretched for hers, seating her and then dropping down beside her, his eyes on the yearbook she held.

"Ryanne?" Redmond crouched down in front of her, his eyes on hers before they dropped to the book. "What are you thinking?"

"That I know exactly who is behind this. And it's not who we think. It's not Mary's family." She flipped through the pages, stopping for a moment to study Redmond in his graduating class before she pointed at a picture. "Him. He's the one. Mary talked about him all the time. They had been dating, I think, on the sly, and then she just stopped talking about him. I never knew why. She never said."

Redmond carefully reached for the book, knowing that if Ryanne was right, he knew the person responsible.

"You're very sure on this?"

She nodded before she hid her face against Shea, his arm around her. Shea watched carefully, studying the picture she had pointed to, before he drew in a deep breath.

"I know him, Redmond. He's been asking me to do photo shoots for him, becoming more and more persistent. I have always refused, not liking the vibes I was picking up from him."

Redmond nodded, his eyes finally dropping to the page, and he drew in a deep breath. "Who would have suspected him?"

Regan peeked over his shoulder. "I would. I never liked him. Neither did Rory or Reilly. They told me once they were glad you weren't friends with him."

"No, we weren't friends. Barely acquaintances." Redmond stood, deep in thought for a moment. "Now, we have to prove this. How?"

"Set a trap. That's how. That's the only way we can do this. We need to do it soon, too. He'll be after us again if we don't."

"How do we do that? We can't involve our parents. Not yet."

"Reilly and Rory won't be left out."

Ideas were tossed back and forth before Ryanne finally stood. "This is getting us nowhere. Let's just go find him.

I'm sure he's sitting somewhere, gloating that we don't know who he is."

"We can't just do that, Ryanne, not without some kind of plan."

She glared at Redmond, then sighed. "And I know Dad would say to pray about it. So let's pray, ask for a plan, and put it into play."

Chapter 42

Ryanne paced in front of the store. They had finally agreed to a plan, and she was the bait, as she put it. Shea had protested vehemently but she had just shaken her head.

"It has to be this way, Shea. He won't come out for anyone else. We all know that."

Now, she was beginning to regret volunteering. She was wearing a wire and had her brothers and sister and Shea nearby. She turned her head slightly, hiding a grin. Shea sat not too far from her, disguised with a cap and fake beard. If it hadn't been so serious, she would have sworn he was enjoying himself. At that moment, he looked up, looked around and then winked at her, driving a giggle from her that she had to contain. Yes, Lord, life will be an adventure with this man. Please let us end this today. None of us can continue.

She turned as she heard footsteps approaching through the open store door and watched as the man appeared. Yes, it was him. The one she suspected but had denied that it was him.

Richard Lewis stood, his eyes on Ryanne in a haughty manner, unsure why she was there but certain she had just played into his hands.

"Ryanne Stuart. To what do I owe the pleasure?"

"Pleasure? I highly doubt that it's a pleasure, Richard. Not with what you've done."

"And just what have I done? You must come in, my dear. It's getting chilly out here." He reached for her arm, stopping when she stepped backwards.

"I will go nowhere with you, Richard Lewis. I know what you did. I know who you are."

"And that would be?"

"Oh, come on, Richard. You know what."

"I do? Really, my dear. You must come in. My sister's here and would like to see you."

She moved away from him, drawing him from the store door, where she could see a woman hovering before she too emerged.

"What does she want, Richard?"

"I have no idea, Adele. I'm trying to get her to come in and we can talk about it where it's warmer."

Ryanne once more shook her head, her eyes on Adele. "Adele Lewis, I knew you were involved. You had to be. In fact, I would say you're the brains behind all this."

"The brains?" Richard began to laugh in a coarse manner. "Not at all. I might as well tell you. You won't live to repeat it to anyone else. Your brother's the reason you ended up kidnapped. I wanted revenge on him. Adele was the one who set it up."

"I don't get it. Why did you want revenge on my brother? And which one of the three would that be?"

"Your oldest brother, Redmond. He had all the marks, the honours, the sports teams that I never had. I tried but always failed. Dad always threw it up to me that your brother was such as success. I settled with Dad years ago. Now it's your turn. Once you're gone, I'll have settled with your brother."

Ryanne looked past him at his sister. "Somehow, that doesn't ring true, Richard. You're not the brains of this."

Adele began to laugh. "She's got you pegged, brother. I was behind it all. I'm the one who convinced our dear departed father that you were no good, that you never would be. He never realized that's what I was up to.   Even today, without me, your store would not succeed."

Richard spun on his sister, advancing towards her, his hands reaching for her neck. Ryanne screamed as that happened, and then a flurry of activity occurred. She was whisked away, safe in Shea's arms, Redmond's hands pushing them into a vehicle. She saw the emergency lights and wondered at that.   She didn't know that Redmond had talked to the detective and arranged it all. He didn't tell her that the wire she wore connected with the police department. He regretted not telling her but knew she would refuse if he had.

Ryanne tore at the wire, pulling it loose, grimacing as the tape pulled at her skin, and thrust it at Redmond, sobs rising within her as she then flung herself into Shea's arms. Shea shared a look with Redmond before the car door closed and they were taken away.

Redmond turned to face the activity, slumping back against his car. Regan approached, reaching to hug him before she too turned and watched as the brother and sister were arrested.

"Where did they go wrong, Redmond?" She knew Reilly and Rory were standing beside them.

"They didn't believe, sis. They left God out of their lives. They wanted it all and failed. He was like that in high school, always wanting whatever it was anyone else had, but never succeeding on his own." Redmond sighed. "Did he really say he killed his father?"

Reilly nodded. "That's what I heard. And I heard his sister confess to setting that up." He looked around, his eyes finding Rory, who nodded.

"Let's go. Ross will find us when he needs to. I want to make sure Ryanne's okay. And then I want to hug my wife for a long time. God has blessed us with parents who believed and taught us right from wrong." Rory walked away on those words.

Chapter 43

A month later, Ryanne, nerves getting the better of her for a moment, stood with her father, her hand tucked into the crook of his elbow, listening to the church pianist playing through the hymns she and Shea had chosen, until she heard the start of the wedding march. Her father looked down at her, his love for his youngest daughter evident on his face.

"You're sure, Ryanne?"

"I am, Dad. He's the one. The one you and Mom prayed for, that Mom wove into my stories and dreams. He's the one I've been waiting for." She looked up at her father, confidence streaming from her. "It's hard for you, I know, to let me go, to realize that I have finally grown up and ready to start the next step in my life."

"You have indeed grown up on me and your Mom, it seems like in no time at all. You are a beautiful, loving, caring, Godly woman. Shea knows that and will treasure you for as long as God gives you. He told me the other day that he thinks of Proverbs 31 when he thinks of you." He reached to kiss her cheek, not willing to walk her down the aisle just then, but knowing Shea was waiting.

"Thank you, Dad. I love you and Mom." She turned her face towards the door and the man waiting for her.

Later that afternoon, she stood, Shea's arms around her as she leaned back on him, watching their family and friends as they mingled in the church basement, where they had chosen to have their reception.

Shea finally spoke. "I love you more and more every day, sweetheart. I have been remiss. I have not told you that enough."

She shook her head. "Words are words. You tell me every day in your actions. They tell me I am loved and cherished." She sobered, the soft smile leaving her face. "Did we really go through all that, Shea?"

"We did. And in a way, I'm glad."

"You are?"

He tightened his arms around her more. "I am. If I hadn't been there that first day, I wouldn't have met you and become the "him" that keeps you safe."

"You are that. And you drove away the dinosaur that haunted me for years. I didn't realize how much that very thought had affected me. I feel for Mary's parents, though. They don't get to celebrate a day like this." She searched through the crowd, finding them talking with her parents. "I am glad they agreed to come. I didn't think they would."

"They talked to me. They weren't going to come, until I told them you wanted them here, that it would help heal your heart as well as theirs. They've gone into counselling with our minister."

"I am so glad, Shea. So very glad." She twisted in his arms, hers around him as he dropped his head and kissed her thoroughly.

"I love you, Mrs. Murdoch. Now, how be we mingle for a bit more?"

"I love you, Mr. Murdoch. And yes, let's mingle. We are truly blessed with family and friends."

Dear Readers:

Thank you for choosing to read Ryanne and Shea's story. Once again, I was just along for the ride. Ryanne was very reticent to tell me her story but finally opened up. The dinosaur? I have no idea where that came from, but I know we all have dinosaurs of some kind in our lives, whether we realize that or not. God is the only one who can keep us safe and take the dinosaurs from us.

We all find ourselves in the midst of storms, some not so bad, others horrible. God is there. He calms the sores. He calms us. He never leaves us.

God Bless

Ronna